Infidelities

Kirsty Gunn published her first novel with Faber in 1994 and since then has written six works of fiction, including short stories and a collection of fragments and meditations. Translated in over twelve territories, and widely anthologised, her books have been broadcast, turned into film and dance theatre, and are the recipients of various prizes and awards, including the Scottish Arts Council Book of the Year. Her 2012 novel *The Big Music* won Book of the Year at the New Zealand Post Book Awards and was shortlisted for the James Tait Black Memorial Prize. She is Professor of Writing Practice and Study at the University of Dundee, where she established and directs the writing programme. She lives in London and Scotland with her husband and two daughters.

Further praise for *Infidelities*:

'"Nobody buys short stories anyway," the writer's husband says, in the fragment that begins Kirsty Gunn's latest collection. And he's right that they can be difficult to sell – unless the writing is as excellent as this . . . In Gunn's world, the surface is never the whole story. Terrific.' Kate Saunders, *The Times*

'Its evocation of a twin yearning for both escape and "absolute arrival" – at once a going out and a coming home – leaves a more cohesive impression than many more disparate collections, and that's an achievement.' Lionel Shriver, *Financial Times*

'This collection is a perfect, witty riposte to that casual dismissal, and a lesson in how much goes on beneath the surface of everyday life . . . Gunn traces these hidden emotional topographies with insight and attentiveness to form and language which marks her previous work . . . delicate, unsettling and revelatory.' Lettie Ransley, *Observer*

'A deft contribution to a growing genre of contemporary fiction that wrestles with itself.' Sophie Elmhirst, *New Statesman*

---

by the same author

RAIN
THE KEEPSAKE
THIS PLACE YOU RETURN TO IS HOME
FEATHERSTONE
THE BOY AND THE SEA
44 THINGS
THE BIG MUSIC

Infidelities

KIRSTY GUNN

FABER & FABER

First published in 2014
by Faber & Faber Ltd
Bloomsbury House
74–77 Great Russell Street
London WC1B 3DA
This paperback edition published in 2016

Typeset by Faber & Faber Ltd
Printed and bound by CPI Group (UK) Ltd, Croydon, CR0 4YY

A CIP record for this book
is available from the British Library

ISBN 978–0–571–30892–7

FSC
www.fsc.org
MIX
Paper from
responsible sources
FSC® C101712

2 4 6 8 10 9 7 5 3 1

For Amelia and Katherine

The start of it . . .

'The stories were always for me to do,' I said.

'What do you mean by that?'

Richard gave me a certain kind of look, a look that came from being up too late and drinking tequila with me at a glamorous bar, but also the kind of look that showed that he knew me very well.

'What do you mean by that?' he said again.

We'd been talking about my short stories, the collection I'd put together and the kinds of short stories I was interested in, though Richard said that they were the kind that would never sell. 'Nobody buys short stories anyway,' he'd said earlier. 'No one thinks there's enough going on.'

'I just mean,' I said, 'that it was always me behind the whole thing. The collection, the idea of those stories I'd written. It was always me, inside them, I was involved. Like the one I was just telling you about, with the woman and her husband, the one that's called "Infidelity" . . . That one. But all of the stories. All of them. I was never going to pretend that they'd just, you know, arrived invisibly on the page. I was always there.'

'Phew,' said Richard. He drained his little tequila glass, and set it down. 'You're there, all right,' he said.

'And I'm also right here.'

'You're the writer, that's for sure,' Richard smiled, that long, slow smile I knew so well. 'You're the one, standing by, just like old James Joyce said.' He tapped his little glass. 'Loitering in some doorway, chewing on his fingernails or whatever—'

'Not chewing,' I said. I took a sip of my own tequila. A hundred per cent agave just like my friend Jennifer from Mexico said is the only kind you should ever have.

'Paring,' I said to Richard, taking another sip. 'Paring his fingernails. That's how Joyce described it, his definition of the artist – standing by – but, sure, you're right, he's there, she's there . . .'

Richard shook his head, he said 'Phew' again. I leaned over and gave him a quick kiss, not on the forehead or cheek, but on his mouth. He closed his eyes then. I closed mine. When I opened them he was looking at me.

Richard. Richard, Richard, Richard. Still himself, still the same man, after all this time, with that same wrecked and gorgeous look I'd been so taken with all those years ago. The same Richard. Drinking too much. Doing everything too much – but as though nothing would ever touch him. As though nothing would come close. He still wore the same kinds of clothes he used to wear when we were together, had the same smell – of smoke and leather and some old fashioned cologne, like some fabulous old club from the eighties. Richard. Richard, Richard. Richard.

'That's the artist standing by, but coldly,' I said, I realised I was talking in a very low voice. I was practically whispering. 'Joyce uses that adverb specifically,' I said. 'So . . . I am not the same. I'm not like him. I'm not coming in on something and using it. I'm not discovering the story, and then writing it down. No. From the beginning, I was there. I'm not cold at all, you see. I'm in the midst.'

By now Richard had my hand in his hand. Very gently, he was stroking one of my fingers with his thumb.

'I should go home,' I said. 'It's late. All this talk of short stories, my collection . . . I should never have told you about any of it. Bringing you into it like this.'

'It's just made you want to go home,' Richard tapped my finger with his thumb. 'But you don't need to go home, not yet. Call your husband, call your children.'

'It's already too late to call them.'

'Well,' Richard said. 'Nevertheless. I want you to sit here, right here where you are. Look at us, in this lovely place . . .' He gestured with a nod of his head, at the restaurant around us, all the yellow lamps and the marble, all the silver buckets and the champagne and the oysters and the ice. 'I want us to stay right here,' he said. 'For now. Please. Don't go just yet.'

'Oh, You . . .' I said.

'No one reads short stories anyhow,' he said, for the second time that night. 'So you don't need to worry about that. We're safe. You and I. And all those things you've written . . . They're only here' – he touched the side of my head – 'and here', and he touched my heart. 'They're nowhere else.'

'They're in the book,' I said. '*Infidelities*. Remember? The whole collection's finished, it's done.' And I leaned over and I kissed him properly then, I kissed him on his lovely mouth.

'I'm glad we've gone out,' he said, after I'd finished. 'Let's stay out. Who knows. Maybe we'll never go home, you and I. Maybe we'll just say we're never coming home again.'

Contents

GOING OUT

A Story She Might Tell Herself 3
Elegy 27
The Scenario 49
Glenhead 63

STAYING OUT

The Highland Stories: 79
   The Father 80
   The Rock 85
   Dirtybed 93
   Ghost 98
The Caravan 109
Foxes 119

NEVER COMING HOME

The Wolf on the Road 129
Tangi 143
Memorial 157
Dick 169
Infidelity 175

GOING OUT

A Story She Might Tell Herself

Bobby had got back late from the pub and said they'd all been talking about it. About this guy, the real thing, he said, from Tibet or someplace like that by the look of him, in the saffron coloured robes and with his little bowl and not speaking a word, just arriving in the midst of the village that day and taking up some kind of position, actually, was the way he'd described it, right there in the covered market under the clock.

And this was . . . What? Twenty years ago? More. Yet even now when all that time has passed and Helen can think about these things, look back upon episodes in her life and reflect upon them – *imagine her way into them,* sometimes, is how it feels – she considers how something did seem to begin for her then, that day, that night, in a way continues to begin. It was there in that phrase of Bobby's: 'Taking up some kind of position'. As though even he, in those words he used, had been aware some-how that the image of a monk from another world could come to sit squarely in the midst of their marriage, sit between the two of them, make it clear how far they were apart.

Helen had just carried on filling the dishwasher while he spoke. Bobby always described anything that happened as though it was his own personal experience – what was happening in the world, in Iraq, say, or in Ireland – as though he'd just come from those places himself when everybody knew he just went to work at the agency and wrote the ads there like he'd always done, stopping each night at 'The Black Lion' for a 'quickie' after he got off the bus, before he came home. He was good at it, holding forth like that. She had put the last of the children's things, their little plates and bottles, into the dishwasher and closed the door, and just let him go on, claiming ownership of something that he hadn't been part of, expecting her not to know the difference. Now he was talking about Tibetan practice and what it was to be a monk in this day and age, what it might mean to have one arriving here in their little Oxfordshire village, settling himself down in the covered market, right in that same place, he said, where Helen had had her organic stand last summer when she'd been in the mood, remember, to do that sort of thing.

Helen sat down herself then. With Bobby at the kitchen table, the dishwasher running and the casserole up behind her on the hob . . . She said, 'Listen, I know.'

She'd always had to do that, to get his attention, would have to sit down and actually face him, speak into his face, have him see her with her mouth moving . . .

4

So she'd said, 'Listen, I know', sitting right there in front of him, and she remembers now the look on his face after she'd spoken, just for a second, maybe, but terrified, terrified.

Then he got up to get another beer from the fridge.

It came from his job, of course. That thing of being used to hearing your own voice, knowing you could convince people with the way you spoke as much as what you said. Ever since Helen had known Bobby he'd described himself that way, like he was proud of it, that Helen would have to turn from what she was doing, take the seat right there before him to intervene in the run of his own conversation. *Am I interesting you at all?* she used to often wonder to herself, in those early months when she was first going out with Bobby, realising that at parties, in certain bars and restaurants, if they were there with a crowd of people he simply wouldn't hear her, wouldn't see her, even. Much less fancy her, she knew, if she didn't put herself right there in his direct line of vision. *Not interesting enough, I guess . . .* she'd thought then, but they'd got together somehow even so, had fun, hadn't they, for a while? Then they'd got married and it was part of what they did together, Helen used to it by then, Bobby talking, her listening to him, moments exactly like that night in the kitchen – except this time she went on to say to him, 'I was there. I saw the monk myself.'

Bobby took a swig of his beer, shrugged, like he thought, 'So?' The bottle he'd just taken out from the fridge already looked near empty, though Helen could hardly remark on that. She'd been sipping away on white wine herself, making sure the glass was always at least half full. Because that was part of their marriage, too, wasn't it? It was what Helen did while she made supper, waiting for Bobby to come home, sorting through the dishes, listening out that she hadn't left the TV on too loud so as to wake Winnie, or wake the boys.

But the fact is, she did know. All about the monk and his little bowl. She'd come from dropping Win at her morning playgroup like she did every morning, leaving the babies tucked up in their baskets in the house without her and with a feeling of anxiety about doing that so she'd be always in a rush to get back to them before they would wake and realise she was gone . . .

Except that she'd been stopped that morning, hurrying up the path by the church, by Elizabeth Ferry from the Rectory saying that this kind of miracle was taking place in the village square. This beautiful Tibetan monk was there, Elizabeth had said, he'd simply arrived amongst them, was sitting now under the clock and would Helen go and sit with him, just for a moment even? She might want to place a few coins in, as Elizabeth put it, 'this amazing earthenware bowl, misshapen, you know, like he's formed it himself out of clay.' She'd talked away, Helen all the time trying to get a word in so she could get back to the twins, but then Elizabeth had gone on to say that everyone in the village, *especially* churchgoers – she'd underlined that *especially* – should go and be with the monk, just for a minute or two,

John had told her, as a way of saying the church supported, no encouraged, other faiths, other prayerful routes to God.

She was like that, Elizabeth. John may have been the Rector in those days, but his wife was the one who 'went out', as she put it, among the parishioners and got to know them, encouraged their little spiritual acts. Helen wonders what she's doing now. The same sort of thing, probably, while John would be indoors like he'd always been, reading, praying. He was quite High, apparently, or had started off that way. Helen had been told that by a neighbour once. That John had been quite keen on that rigmarole with incense and the saints. But since she'd been going along to church, not that regularly but often enough to try to feel part of things, she could only see him as being more of a kind of Presbyterian, the sort she was used to, really, especially being married to someone like Elizabeth who was always talking about Islam and Buddhism and other religions. It was children, it occurs to Helen now, who he often talked about when he stood up in front of them on a Sunday. About children's imagination being a sort of faith in itself. What a lovely idea that is, she thinks now. Not at all the kind of thing you'd expect from someone who'd once been quite High. Or was it? Back then, Helen had supposed, that kind of talk was all about getting more people in the pews, but thinking about it now . . . Well, maybe John's interest in mystery and the imagination had always been just the same as loving incense and candles . . . Probably after all it was the same. Still, that morning it had felt strange. To have

Elizabeth stopping her the way she did and saying, pretty much, that it was John this time telling people what to do. *Especially churchgoers*, is what Elizabeth had said. No wonder they'd been full of it in the pub. Everyone must have been full of it – shy John speaking out, Elizabeth galvanising the whole village to act in a special sort of way.

Helen herself had looked at her watch and said 'okay' to her, 'I can do five minutes', aware of the eight-month-old babies sleeping at home and having an image of them, wrapped up like little packages in their baskets, sleeping for now, but who knows what could happen if they awoke. Still, she'd said 'okay'. She'd been 'Showing Willing' – that phrase of Bobby's they'd started using since they came here from London, since Winnie was born, and then the twins, and she'd found herself having to try to fit into village life. 'Showing Willing' meant that she would do what she had to do to be like the others, the other women in the village, be prepared to be, at least – that's what Bobby said. He was the one who'd come up with the phrase for her, as a way of getting past all that big-city snobbery about people who lived in English villages and he'd been delighted with it, the way the words maintained an upper hand while doing all that institutional friend-making that was necessary in these small conservative places that were an hour or two away from London and on the commuter circuit, maybe, but deep in the heart of the Home Counties even so. It was all about being 'dependable', learning to – how had Bobby put it? – 'act local'. As though, Helen thinks now, he knew anything about acting 'local' when he was as much a

Londoner as she was – but she'd ended up showing willing even so. Bobby stopping into 'The Black Lion' every night didn't count. Because showing willing had meant much much more than simply being with people, hadn't it? It had meant doing things that sometimes made her feel silly and shy but still she did them to show she was friendly, like that organic stall the year before all this happened, when she'd set up a trestle table and sold potatoes and salad vegetables and fruit. She'd been aware of herself then as willing indeed, the very picture of making an effort and being jolly as she chatted to her neighbours and counted out change. A glowing pregnant woman is how she'd wanted to see herself back in those days. Laying out before her the healthy and lovely foods, her little toddler playing beside. Showing willing in the covered market every Friday until she'd got too exhausted by the weight she was carrying, the exhausting feel of the twins growing bigger and bigger inside her, and she'd had to give the market up and stay, pretty much, alone and relieved at home.

Helen had known then – she sees this clearly now – that giving up the market was when she'd realised that deep down she'd never be dependable the way Bobby had planned. That she could show willing all she wanted but that didn't necessarily mean she could become one particular kind of person, the kind who didn't change, want other things. She sensed the other women in the village were like that though, cheerful and fixed in their habits. They didn't dart furtively in and out of church as though they didn't quite belong there; they stayed around and

drank instant coffee afterwards, they ran church commit-
tees and fairs. It was the same at the toddler group where
she took Win, where she was surrounded by these women
so comfortable in their role as 'Mum', with their gardens
and their husbands and their quiet nights in front of the
TV . . . But how could Helen have ever felt she was fixed
in that safe and secure way when all the time she had a
kind of panic, that rose up gradually in the day, got better
in the evening when she poured her first glass of wine,
but then came back in the morning, dark and lusty, to
claim her.

She sees now that she was nothing but change in those
days – one person here, meeting Elizabeth by the church
hall, another there, getting Bobby into bed at night, making sure she herself had a huge glass of water by her bed
for if she were to wake feeling dehydrated and sick. Of
course she wasn't dependable, she knew it then like she
knows it now. The only difference is it was covered up
then, by the habit of Bobby, of looking after him and
being with him. So the house had been tidy and the twins
and Winnie well cared for and clean and no one would
have ever known, would they, that beneath it all was this
other life – rushing and uncertain and frightening, even –
with a feeling in it that anything could happen, anything.
It was why she'd married Bobby, wasn't it? To try to protect herself against that feeling? It was why she listened to
him, let him go on and on. As though she might turn her
life into a story told by someone else – one of his stories
in fact – like a story might calm a person and quieten

them in the dark, fill the void with words and phrases and sentences that they might go to sleep.

Like that word: 'Dependable'. Back then, Helen thinks now, her mind had been full up with those kinds of words and thoughts: That they might make her into somebody who would 'show willing' and do the right thing. So of course she'd gone down to the covered market that day as she'd promised and sure enough there he was, the monk, right there by the clock just like Elizabeth had said. He was sitting in the lotus position wearing yellow robes and with the little bowl . . . *Taking up some kind of position.* Only this time it wasn't Bobby talking. It wasn't one of his stories. Because Helen had seen the monk. She'd seen him herself.

That moment comes in on her now, like then. For hadn't it seemed, at first, impossible to believe?

He'd been like a statue, sitting in that dainty way, his head bowed, the bare feet curved up neatly and tucked into each other in his lap and that smile on his face like you see in all the travel brochures to Tibet. Like the smile on the faces of the monks when there'd been the show of Tibetan art at the V&A and then the other one at the Met when she'd been living in New York that time, staying with an old friend of her mother's who was taking care of her, really, while Helen had been trying to straighten things out in her life, trying to decide whether or not she'd even marry Bobby, and they'd flown monks in from a monastery somewhere in India to make those sand mandalas on the floor . . .

But how much of all that, though, came back to her the moment when she saw the monk – Helen can't be sure. In a way it's because thinking now about these details, of that day, and what followed . . . The whole act of remembering starts to bring up all kinds of other memories too. Yet, though she can't be sure if it felt that that part of her life came back to her so completely in that moment of seeing the monk, of remembering that time of living in New York . . . Well, all she can think is that it feels like that now. As though her whole life, somehow, came up and surrounded him. Who she'd been. What she'd done. Remembering the way she'd felt so free in New York but also so scared – realising that she was on the verge of deciding something that needed thought and care but rushing towards it as though with her eyes closed, rushing forward amidst all the clubs and the bars and the partying, running around New York and knowing Bobby was over in London, waiting, waiting . . .

Certainly what she was aware of at the time was the way that day, that morning, each detail around the monk – the dark stones and brickwork of the village building, the gilt detail around the face of the clock, the fresh blue china colour of the summer sky, early and fresh and really like polished china because there'd been rain last night – seemed to charge itself, Helen thinks now that's exactly it, the phrase, 'charge itself', each detail lending her its full and significant meaning. And set against these things, these *things,* the *thingness,* if you like, of building stones and of sky, was the vivid colour of saffron robes, the little earthen bowl, pale straw of the sitting mat . . . These elements of the monk that seemed on another plane altogether, ethereal, even though they were right there in front of her, come out of a place way beyond herself, unknown to her entirely, of hope or faith or dream.

Something started for her then. She had the strong instinct which of course she immediately quelled to put her hands together to form her hands into a prayer position like the monk was doing, to extend herself towards him that way . . . But she hadn't done that, not anything crazed or needy. Instead, she'd managed, after all the initial feelings of belief and disbelief and of wonder, to be exactly as Elizabeth had suggested. She'd approached the monk, gently put a few coins and a crumpled note into the begging bowl at the corner of the mat, and said, slowly but in a very safe, English way, 'Welcome.'

The man looked into her eyes. He didn't speak.

That 'welcome' must have sounded strange yet Helen hadn't felt foolish about it, or even embarrassed – really it was as though she'd entered a kind of dream. Everything was quiet, set. There was a stillness in the air, around the monk, that Helen was part of – as though the stillness had entered her, was part of her. A feeling Helen recognises now in a way she couldn't then as calm. It was only when Margaret Cockburn from three doors down arrived, and came up to the monk and said 'Welcome' pretty much in the same way Helen had, that it was as if she remembered, with a start, the twins back home on their own, and she rushed away, arriving at the house with her heart like a roaring engine as she tore up the stairs, three at a time. There were the boys though, just as she'd left them, quiet and placid and only starting to move when she leaned over them and startled them with her noisy, ragged breath. She stayed there some time, standing over them, watching them, listening to the small sucking noises they made as they opened and closed their mouths, getting ready for their next feed . . . But even as she did so by then all she was thinking about was the monk in the village and that moment of her standing before him and feeling everything was still, like a painting she could stay standing in front of and as long as she stood there would never feel panic again or terror or deep, deep despair.

All that day she'd thought of nothing else. Remembering that feeling. Trying to get it back. So though she couldn't really understand why she would need to look at the monk again, nevertheless she knew she'd have to – so she bundled the boys up into the pram and used picking up Winnie from playgroup as her excuse to go back to the village.

'There's an interesting spaceman come to visit us,' she'd said to her daughter, meeting her at the church hall door. 'Shall we go and see him, you and I?'

Winnie looked up at her, her hair tumbled from her morning's play and with that lovely heat coming off her, Helen always felt, like a feeling of her daughter's certainty, her little body so solid and fixed and sure of itself in the world.

'Can John John and Barney come too?' she asked. She peered down at the twins, made a face at them and they twisted with delight.

'Of course,' Helen said.

'Okay.'

Which was how Helen had done it, made it seem like the most ordinary thing that she would have to go back to the same place where she'd been that morning, just to stand there again. She'd had a bag with her to do some shopping if she wanted to, as though she might be going to the square for that reason, keeping her daughter with her as a sort of alibi, to buy her an ice cream or a bag of sweets – because where would she have been sometimes in that period of her life without Winnie and that sturdy little body of hers? Set beside her in the street or in a shop and giving her a reason to be there, giving her something to do? Like a daughter's hand can always hold on to a mother's hand to keep the mother safe. And where, Helen thinks, would she be without that hold, even now, where?

She'd looked down at Winnie, to see if she'd thought it was odd that they weren't going home straight away, but Winnie just stuck her thumb in her mouth and peered around Helen to wiggle her fingers at the boys as Helen pushed them along in the pram. The twins kicked and twisted again and let out little shrieks of laughter.

'You know, he is like a real spaceman, Win,' Helen said. 'He's wearing a yellow dress, though, so more like Jesus.'

Winnie nodded, the thumb stayed in her mouth. Really, it was the time for her sandwich and a glass of milk and then her afternoon nap, Helen thought. They should be going home. Still she swung the pram around and back towards the square, thinking that if she could just see him, the monk, one more time, just put him again in the line of her vision, have that feeling that she'd had before of calmness and of still, keep the image of seeing him with her like a photo – she wouldn't even necessarily have to go up close . . . But when they got there the crowd was so thick around him that she couldn't even a catch a glimpse of his yellow robe. Then one of the boys started to cry, John, and Winnie was saying, 'I'm *hungry.* I'm *hungry*, Mummy' – so Helen gave up on the idea and they went home.

That had all been in the morning, and then, hours later, there was Bobby, sitting in front of her telling her about it. The crowd gathering, who'd been there with the monk, who hadn't, what they'd said. In a way, Helen had thought, looking at him, you could say it was quite lovely, his enthusiasm for the story, the way Bobby seemed so involved, but in another way she also knew exactly how much he'd been drinking by the look in his eyes.

He grinned at her. 'Not every day, is it? We get something like this happening in olde-worlde middle England? Middle Earth more like it. It must have given you a shock, darling. Didn't it? When you're the one who *saw* him, after all.'

He'd fixed her with his eyes as he said that – his pretty, deep blue eyes with that dark, private look that no one else could see except her. Which showed his hours of nights spent alone in the kitchen with a whisky bottle, or knocking back vodka miniatures before meeting clients for lunch . . . It was all part of the same story. Bobby's story. *We're in this together*, the look said. *You are the only one.* Helen turned away.

'But I'm talking to you,' Bobby had said.

'I know.' She could hear it in his voice then, the change. If anyone were to come into the kitchen now, a neighbour, a friend, he'd be jolly and charming and he'd be able to stay like that for another couple of hours, but here on his own, with just her . . .

'I *said* I'm talking to you.'

'What, then?' Helen stood up from the table.

'I'm saying that I don't care what you saw or didn't see. That someone needs to take charge here. Himalayas or no Himalayas.'

'I'm sorry,' Helen said, 'I didn't hear you, I was listening out for the boys.'

'I said your monk is in the woods tonight, he should be there now. And I don't care if he is used to it. This is England, for godsake, not the damn Indian mountains . . .'

Helen stopped – felt herself stopping, rather, is closer to what she means. Because she had picked up a wooden spoon and was stirring the meat in the casserole, she was doing something, but it was as if she wasn't, as if she wouldn't know how. There was the table, the empty bottles. The lit kitchen, dark bedrooms upstairs where the children were sleeping. There was Bobby standing, slowly, carefully opening the fridge door to reach inside.

And there she was, unable to go forward, unable to do anything at all.

Then she started to speak, 'I had no idea—' but Bobby interrupted her.

'Oh, yeah,' he continued as though she'd been in on the conversation from the beginning, had been listening to everything he'd said, as though she'd been there in the pub all along right beside him. 'Someone said, an interpreter or someone, that's what he was doing. That after sunset he was going to go up into the Ten Shilling Wood behind Parson's Farm and sleep there, spend the night there on his little damn mat.'

Helen looked out the kitchen window across the garden beyond the paddock and there were the woods. She imagined that tiny, delicate man she'd seen earlier in the day walking into them, the sun going down behind the mass of branches all around him. She saw the way the last of the sun's light might filter between the trees' leaves, like bright coins flashing, dazzling his eyes, but quickly fading, the ground deepening and softening underfoot as he went further and further in.

She had to find him. She became aware of it that minute. That she had to go out there into the woods, up on to the hill, go through the woods and look for him. Though it seemed the most crazy thing in the world, still she had to, somehow, for some reason, find him. For *what* reason, though? Helen even now still can't figure that part out. As a sort of recovery? Redress? To get back that feeling she'd had in the morning of stillness and of calm? Like she'd wanted to go back later that morning to see the monk again and claim that feeling then and there'd been too many people there and she couldn't see? Or was it more, as if by doing something unknown to her and peculiar, really – looking in the woods for a strange, unknown man – she could prove to herself the strength of what she'd felt that morning, get it back like an act of faith somehow? She didn't know. Still she doesn't. But she'd turned away from the window and the sunset was already blanching from the sky and what had Bobby said: 'After sunset'? And she'd thought: I have to go there now.

'I think you should.'

'What?'

Bobby's voice had interrupted her.

'What did you say?'

'I said I think you should go into the woods to find him. Your monk, I mean. Show him some English hospitality, for godsake. You and your village ladies. I left money behind the bar so there's a bed for him at 'The Lion' at least. I thought of doing that, you see. I'd thought of that at least. So go and find him, if he means so much to you that you *saw* him after all. Maybe you even, I don't know, all you ladies, touched his robes. But just go. While I'm eating,' Bobby said. 'While I go to bed.'

Helen had nodded slowly. She didn't look at Bobby, she couldn't bear to, and she didn't say anything straight away. She reached for a plate, ladled gravy on to it and meat and potatoes, set it down in front of him along with a knife and fork.

Then she said 'Thank you' to him, very quietly. As though, whether he'd intended it or not, whether she was to understand those words of his the way she did or not, whether they came from the part of him that understood her and knew what she was like, or whether he meant them as a threat, that he was testing her and that it was an offer that would quickly turn . . . He was giving her something. There in the midst of the children, in the house, with their sons asleep in their baskets, Winnie in her little bed . . . In the midst of those rooms, that kitchen here with its casserole cooking in its juices and the dishes that were too many to fit into the dishwasher piled in the sink, and the vegetables and the salad she'd meant to go together as part of the meal but were still sitting on the bench, in the midst of all this, the bottles and the beer Bobby was drinking and the wine in her own glass, the pale colour of it and needing to keep its own particular pale colour in her glass so she could be with her husband at all, be with him and look after him, with his blue eyes, be happy enough with what he did to be able to stay . . . As though in the midst of all of it she'd whispered 'Thank you' to him as though he really had given her something, as though he were letting her go.

She reached for the keys where they hung on their hook behind the kitchen door, turned back for a minute to see Bobby at the kitchen table before she stepped outside. But in those few seconds he'd gone, his head down over his plate like an animal, shovelling in great forkfuls of beef and gravy and the weight and angle of his body at the table unbalanced, as if any second he was going to fall.

*

It took Helen only minutes to back the car down the drive and turn up the road towards the farm. There at the third gate on the left was the little track road that ran up into the woods, and Helen turned the car in there and drove up a way until she could see the opening at the side of the road where you could pull in and park. Not many people in the village or anywhere seemed to use this place. It was supposed to be the official entrance to a proper track for ramblers and serious walkers but when she and Bobby had come here, just after they'd moved and Winnie was still a baby, when they'd still believed they might do things like that all the time as a family, make picnics, go for walks, well, though they hadn't even got out of the car, they'd seen no walkers then, no cars. Nor afterwards, when she'd come here herself a few times, just on her own, or with Winnie, she remembered once, she didn't know why, this was well before the twins were born, there'd been no cars here either and no feeling, when she'd ventured into the woods, of a path or a track. Maybe you needed a map, or someone to tell you exactly where to go. Whenever she'd started into the woods then, she'd had a threatening sense of the way the opening in the trees had closed behind her and she'd had to come back out after just a few minutes, following the way she'd gone, otherwise she knew she'd have been lost.

Now though, she simply parked the car, and, leaving the keys in the ignition, opened the door and, without bothering to close it behind her, walked straight in. At once, the act of doing that, going into the woods alone, this time of the evening, to search for a monk did not seem strange or curious at all. These woods in this part of Oxfordshire are ancient beech and ash and acorn, closely planted, so once inside, amongst them, there's the illusion of a hundred little pathways going every which way, each one inviting you further in amongst the trees in a way that makes being here inevitable. Maybe one of these is the path for the ramblers, intended by whoever it was set out the carpark, went to the trouble of erecting a sign, 'Ten Shilling Wood Walk: circular/ten miles', and giving instructions for views along the way and clearings. For now though, to Helen, any one of these paths may be a path or simply another way of being lost and either way it's the same; each one seems to come for her and offer itself to her as a way for her to come further and further in.

There is nothing but silence in these trees. In the fading light the paleness of the tree trunks, beige and grey and violet, rises up around her like people in a crowd parting to let her through. There's the smell of wet earth and leaves and the greenness of the leaves, the haze of green that seems to come from them is like a kind of breath.

I could be anywhere here.

She thinks, *anywhere,* imagining the yellow robes flittering just ahead, in and out of the trees, like wings. Where to begin to find him? She walks ahead a few paces, turns, traces a new direction. Still the branches full of green leaves hold back the sky, keep it from coming down over her head, still the trees step back, reassemble themselves, to let her pass by. Her foot catches on something, a root, some sort of viney tendril, and when she leans down to unwind it from her sandal she notices how wet the ground is, how all the time she's been walking her sandals have become thick and clogged with buttery lumps of mud. She takes them off altogether and leaves them. There are all the textures of the forest floor she can feel now underfoot, of leaves and twigs and the softness of mulch and she walks on, enjoying the sensation of her feet shaping themselves with each step to the contours of the ground, seeming to know which way to go.

Anywhere . . .

She realises she's walking quite quickly this way. And that sound she can hear, it's the sound of her own breath like she's running, panting. Her heart beating.

Anywhere . . .

Rising, beating. Walking faster all the time faster, like she really could be running now. The feeling of being on the run from something, from someone, or running towards them, the feeling of being completely lost. For she is lost, but she knows it as surely as she knows that her bare feet are carrying her onwards, careless, that her body is happy here, the ground against the skin of her bare feet, disappeared from that other place, from that kitchen and the person in that kitchen and the children who are in the room above that kitchen, and slipped into these woods, become a white shape in the disappearing light, in the growing darkness, flitting in and out of the trees, towards a scrap of yellow fabric, maybe, that glimpse of saffron colour amongst the trees, but it's as though forgotten, what it was she came for, what she's looking for even as she runs on, seeking, towards it.

She didn't find him. Later, she couldn't even work out how long she'd been in there, in the trees, cutting from pathway to pathway, couldn't remember when the last of the light leached from the sky and the violet colour that was left deepened and mixed itself in with black. She couldn't remember, either, at what point she stopped feeling herself to be looking for the monk who, she'd been told, crazily, was going to be asleep in the woods that evening. All she remembers is that she went in looking for him and she came out having forgotten, for a time completely, who she was, what she was doing, why she'd gone in.

That in itself had been a kind of miracle, she would reflect much later, when telling this story to herself, her story, as though to someone who might write it down, putting in all the details, one line following another line. How she managed to get out of the woods that night, find her way back to the car and how, in the instant of seeing it there, the inside light on in the darkness because of leaving the door open, and you might say, making the air around seem darker because of the illumination, still she didn't feel the huge relief she might have felt as follows a panic, but in fact the opposite was true. For the sky didn't seem dark, or the earth wet or sharp with stones and roots, nothing treacherous at all, in fact, to make her feel there'd been anything strange or odd about what she'd been doing.

It's true, none of it had scared her, she thinks, when she looks back over these events. Being in that shadowy place, somewhere that was unknown to her, where she may or may not have encountered a holy man whose language she did not speak . . . What exactly was she planning to say to him, anyway, if she'd found him? What, if anything, was she going to do? None of that had been part of it, actually, had seemed important – only that inevitable sense of entering the woods, then the feeling once inside them of flight, of letting her feet take her, at first deeper and deeper in, and then out again to the car, a light, a key.

The engine started straight away and Helen drove home, went quietly inside the house where all the lights were on, empty bottles on the table and the smeared plate . . . Bobby's dirty things. Mechanically she tidied the remains of him away, switched off the lights, made her way into her daughter's room. There was no question of being with her husband now. That thought came to her like the memory of yellow cloth in the woods – real but not real, imagined but also seen . . . *Like a vision.* That's what it had been. She'd heard herself say the words. *A vision.* What she'd been part of. What the whole day had been. Quietly, she got undressed down to her T-shirt and pants, checked on the boys quickly and slid into bed beside her child. She held Winnie snug into her, against her belly, felt the weight of her warm breathing body. In seconds she was asleep.

In the middle of the night, though, or so it seemed, she was awoken by Winnie's sharp cry. The child was sitting bolt upright on the bed clutching herself, the covers tumbled off. 'There's blood!' She was pointing. 'Look! Blood!'

For there, marked like viscera, was a smear of dark across the sheet, gone from the middle right down to the bed's depth, and for a minute Helen thought her daughter was right – the slippery colour of it, the thick womblike consistency in the dark, old and womanly and primal, like bridal stain or miscarriage or afterbirth, matter come from deep within herself . . .That it really was blood. In the dark that's how it looked. But it was the mud from her feet, from where she'd been, what she'd been doing, that was in the bed with her. It was earth mixed with water that was on the sheet, that was the mark all through the bed that had scared Winnie so – although it could have been blood, Helen realises, years and years later, and Winnie grown up now and the boys, and Bobby far, far away. That it was part of herself come out of herself, a change that occurred in one day, one night, that made everything different to how it had been, so the mark that was left could have been like blood. May as well have been.

*

Elegy

The flowers had all come home to roost in the magnolia trees along the Euston Road. It was springtime in London. A song, Elisabeth thought, the moment she saw the pink petals fluttering in the branches: Springtime in London. Magnolia trees. A song.

Of course it wasn't warm, she'd registered that the moment she'd stepped out of the Edinburgh train on to the platform at King's Cross. It was freezing, actually, outside on the taxi rank waiting her turn, there was a bitter wind and her winter coat felt thin. Yet speeding along in the cab a few minutes later, looking through the window after all this time away at a sky that could mean any season at all, that dove-belly grey of the city she used to know so well . . . There it was, all right, in the pale colour of the flowers ruffled up together, perched amongst the bare branches: Spring again, she'd thought, even now. *It could be spring. Let it be.*

The taxi seemed to take a long time, though, even with all this daydreaming, these thoughts of homecoming, remembering. It didn't seem to be very busy on the road, but whatever it was, the cab stopping, starting, red lights every couple of minutes and then a queue formed on the flyover to take the turning for Westbourne Park, it made their progress slow enough . . . So maybe there was a lot of traffic after all and she'd just forgotten, after the years in Scotland, what London was like, what the congestion of people here was like. The cars banked up as they came off the Westway, and stopped – all the taxis and four-wheel drives that everyone seemed to favour nowadays, the motorcycles and the vans and the buses . . . It was unnecessary, is how it seemed, to be taking this long when she was close enough to the flat after ten minutes or so in the cab and Elisabeth normally would get out and walk if only she was feeling stronger. In the old days she would have. *But, hey.* That was then, right? This was now. And if she was back on the island she wouldn't even be thinking about traffic, about any of this. Whether she could walk, couldn't walk, gauging the progress of a London cab against her own perfectly good stride that always had served her well on her beloved hills, the round walk she used to take along the seafront every morning, and up along the lookout before cutting down to the house . . . But that was then, now, too. The island, her life there. Back then she'd never needed to think of strong or not strong, about any of this. She'd be . . . Just . . .

Well, forget about how she'd be. Let it be spring, instead. Nothing more. Just magnolia trees. And blossoms. A song in the key of – G major. Yes, that would do it. Or A. A lovely big glissando to start and then straight into something bright and long and easy for the alto voice. Just think about a song like that, and leave the rest, don't let thoughts drift on to anything else. So it took a little longer to get from one place to another, so there were a lot of people here, all wanting, just like she was, to get from one place to somewhere else . . . That's big cities, right? She used to know about them, remember? 'You're not on your hill now,' Edward would say to her, if he was here. 'Look at me, darling. Look at me. Everything's going to be all right, okay? Look at me. I promise you.'

Yeah, well. Elisabeth smiles. Edward and his 'Look at me'. He'd done the best he could and she loved him for it, loved him, for his steady way with things. The fact that he never once, not once, acted scared or weak or worried. He'd just behaved as he always did: Take one thing at a time, don't jump the gun, rush to conclusions. So one doctor had one opinion, so they'd ask another one. That's what he'd said, right back at the beginning. And there were specialists, people who knew more than those giving out the diagnoses, half the time, you just had to find out who they were, how to get to them. It would all be okay. So she'd looked back at him, let him hold her gaze with his fine, steady gaze: 'All right?' he'd said. 'I promise you.' And the letters came in, and the calls, and there were appointments fixed in all the big hospitals in Scotland, the research hospitals . . . And she'd had the first round of surgery, and then the second . . .

She'd call him the minute she got into the flat. Both of them had had the same idea, after all, to give London a go now they'd tried everything else and he'd wanted to come with her only it had been her who'd said she'd rather travel down on her own. He'd want to know, of course he would, how the journey had been, how she was feeling. He seemed a long way away, already, somehow, Edward. A long way away, and another life. 'I can be on a plane the minute you need me,' he'd said. So she would call him, she would, the minute she got in – and yet . . .

'Well, we'll see.'

'What's that, love?'

The cab driver half turned his head, catching her eye in the rear vision mirror. 'Didn't get that, you were saying?'

'Oh, nothing.' Elisabeth looked out the window, the trees were bare again, this part of Paddington where they were now. No sign of those glorious flowers. 'Only I was thinking . . .' she said, bringing herself back into the present, 'The traffic. Has it been this bad in London for long? I mean, I remember it, but—'

'Not familiar, eh?'

The driver gave out a laugh. He was still half turned towards her – there was that phrase, wasn't there, about only having one eye on the road? That was him. 'Careful,' Elisabeth wanted to say, although she herself never drove any longer, never drove on the island, why would she need to. Still – *Careful.*

'But I suppose we're not moving that fast, are we?' she said to him now.

'Never, love. It's London.' He shook his head. 'Not fast now, not later. Not any time of day. Where you from, anyhow?'

'Scotland.'

'Yeah?'

'A small island, way off to the west.'

'Phew!' the guy whistled. 'Up there, eh? So what you want to come here for, then? Too quiet for you, is it? Up there? You fancied a visit or what?'

'Oh, I'm going to be staying,' Elisabeth said. 'I'm coming back, you see. I used to live here. So yes, I'm planning to stay. For a while, I mean.'

'Yeah?'

'Yeah.'

There was a prick, then, a sting. *Idiot.* That was from not concentrating, letting herself drift. Not seeing the blossoms. *Idiot*, twice. Think about the song. She wasn't going to cry.

'You're here for Easter then, aren't you?' said the driver. 'You've come in the nick of time, starting yourself off with a holiday and all. You got friends here? Family?'

'Something like that.' Elisabeth no longer felt like crying. She just wanted to get to the flat now, off the flyover and back into Westbourne Park and home.

Home.

That was a strange thought, though. With the tenant only just having moved out and Elisabeth herself not having been at the flat for years, so it was hardly home, was it? But, 'Just call her and explain,' Edward had said.

'Alice will understand.' And she had, too, lovely Alice Fairburn, the perfect tenant, Elisabeth always said. How lucky they were to have her. It seemed like it was only hours after Edward had spoken to Alice and she'd moved out to her sister's in Islington, all her clothes, bits and pieces, everything. 'Take it back for as long as you need it,' she had said to Edward, he'd told Elisabeth that she'd put it that way. With no pressure, no decisions that had to be made. *Because it won't be for long*, Elisabeth thinks now, had thought then, too, straight away. Coming in as she was that minute to the street where she used to live and it looking just the same as it always did and the trees out here, too, the magnolia tree by her own front door in blossom . . . Despite what she'd told the driver, it's what she thought as the cab had turned the corner . . . She was back for a visit, after all. She wasn't planning to stay.

Yet the place was so familiar. That feeling of being back, once she was inside the front door. It was lovely how certain houses did that to you. For though it had been several years, more than several, since she'd last been in Circus Gardens, the moment she turned the key in the lock and the key turned, and she stepped into the front hall . . . All of the past rushed up to meet her then and it really was like no time had passed between then and now, no time. There were the wooden stairs before her, some of the risers bashed and half painted as they'd always been; there the landing at the top, the long window giving on to the little terrace where she used to sunbathe . . . Alice hadn't changed a thing. The window – just the same. The terrace. And how many years ago was that, anyway? Since she'd been that girl sitting out there in the sun with a book and a tube of suncream? *Life is long, after all. See?* Edward coming up on her from behind, as she was sitting out there in the sun, putting his arms around her. 'So this is what you do all day, is it?' he'd be saying. 'When you tell me you're composing?' – and her laughing and saying it was true, she'd written this piece or had a draft for that. Or she was thinking about something, on a larger scale perhaps. 'What is it this time, an opera?' he would say. 'No, just a string quartet.' 'Ah, right. Of course. A string quartet.' Laughing again, and kissing her.

So . . .

Life is long.

There was the window. The little terrace.

See?

And then, lugging her bag, up the stairs, past the landing, past the kitchen, there was the sitting room, too, just as she had left it, with the grand piano still there – of course it would be. She went over and touched a key, middle C. Dusty to the touch but clear sounding. She ran up and down the scale a couple of times, then into D, and E, all the way through the octave, and then the bass hand. Out of tune by now, the piano would be, but not so bad. She sat down at the bench. She'd done so much of her early work on that piano, even now she thinks, lying up here in bed, how it seems to wait downstairs for her like a friend. Going through the scales again, C major, then D, then E, then F . . . And the piano responding to her touch, just as it always had. Then F sharp minor. And ouch. That note. In particular. It would take a lot of tuning after all to put that note straight again – but Elisabeth took off her coat even so and played a little Chopin Prelude, and it didn't sound so terrible, did it? And after that a piece she'd written herself called 'Circus Gardens'. She went to play it through but then, in the midst of the first passage, before she could finish, the feeling again, of the prick, the sting. And having to put her hand up to her mouth to press back the force of emotion. *Idiot. Idiot.* Circus Gardens. It was unlikely she was going to see Edward again.

Edward.

His idea to get the piano in the first place. He always had the best ideas. It was Edward who said 'Let's buy it' when they first saw the piano, the perfect size of it, in the saleroom. 'You'll play it but it's for both of us,' he'd said – because it was to be a kind of a prize, sort of, a reward. For the first piece she'd written that had been properly performed, for the novel he'd published. 'We're in this together,' Edward had said. 'Let's get it. This can be the beginning.'

Remember?

'Of course I remember.' She speaks the words out loud, to the window, to the blue sky. The piano is downstairs, quiet now, but waiting.

'I remember it all.'

She started to pick out another tune, something else from the same time, those early years when they'd only just moved in here – but stopped. Really she should have arranged to have had the piano looked after. Alice was never going to do that. Alice wasn't a musician, it wouldn't occur to her to have it played regularly, properly tuned. Maybe they should have had someone else here who would have taken more care – but then, Elisabeth and Edward had never been the kind of couple who thought things through that way, they let things pass, let things go. And so it was years since Elisabeth herself had even played it, years and years, and she'd been young and well, in love and strong and all the future outside the window, part of the blue sky, like it might go on for ever. Like an octave you might spin out from under your fingers and it would go on and on up the scale, and on and up and never reach the end. All the notes of the keyboard and beyond, more, still there to play, the white notes, the black notes, whole notes, accidentals, on and on . . . As though playing all the way through time, Elisabeth thinks, and here she is now . . . *Here she is* . . . As though already the end is here but really it's all part of the same octave, the end of the tune within the notes because there's no beginning, lying here, and in the same way no end either, so that's all right, then, close your eyes. The lovely past with its music all around you and the sun on the terrace and your legs bare and stretched out before you and the heat beating down on the top of your head, Edward's arms around you . . . Close your eyes . . . Because . . .

Here she is . . .

And she remembers thinking that on that day, too, when she'd arrived at the flat, was standing there by the piano. 'Here I am,' she'd said to herself then, the moment she'd dreaded come to rest around her, after she'd finished playing, in the silence. Really, she thought then, it wasn't so bad. To be alone. To have decided alone what she was going to do. To have come down off her hill. Not so bad.

'Go back,' Edward had said. 'Set your mind at rest. Have the tests. See the people at the Wigmore Hall, let them arrange for you to do the Adagio for them like you want it. Have some time, do that. I'll be here. When you're ready, I'll come and get you. I'll be waiting.'

Because she'd kind of known, hadn't she? From the moment she decided to come back here on her own? That it was all down to her from now on, that she wouldn't see Edward again. From the moment the doctor called that last time, and he'd asked her to come in; how his rooms in Edinburgh seemed colder than before and there was no nurse there with him this time, and how he came to the door to meet her . . . Because after they'd spoken, her first thought then was: I can fit it all in. Get back to London. Hear them do the Adagio, be there at the Wigmore to hear it. Organise the legal stuff, the medical stuff. I've enough time. In a couple of months, early spring, there was time then to fit it all in. There'd be rehearsals, she'd told Edward, and she wanted to be at some of the rehearsals, to meet the conductor who she'd never met, and, she told him, she would see the specialist then that they'd both talked about, have the tests he offered and the new treatment, and Edward had called Alice and fixed it with her and Alice had said to 'take as long as you need, no bother'. She had a sister in Islington, she'd said; Elisabeth could just go back to the old flat and settle right in . . .

The diagnosis had always been fixed.

That last appointment, the doctor coming to the door to meet her – what was that phrase of his, in the consulting rooms at Edinburgh? 'We know where we stand' – Elisabeth thought of him, David someone, as she sat at the piano, in Circus Gardens, in London. David Airdrie, that was his name. It was as though he was from another life. And another life ago again when she'd stood with Stewart Campbell in his consulting rooms in the village, in the little medical centre she'd barely been to before all this – the odd antibiotic, one year a bad flu – and there was Stewart using the same expression, near enough. That they would need to do some scans, that she would have to see someone else. On the mainland, in Inverness, but Edinburgh preferably, so they could 'know where we're at', had been his phrase. Elisabeth had been aware then, in his choice of words that day, that people only used that kind of language when talking about something more serious than an operation. An operation, after all, was something to prepare for and recover from. There was a timeline present in 'operation' that wasn't present in 'know where we're at'. 'Know where we're at', she'd thought then, has no timeline at all. So by the end of the summer when she'd seen the second specialist, and what was his name, too, a friend of Stewart Campbell's wasn't he? and he'd given the second opinion and the date was fixed for the first round of surgery a year ago . . . The language was clear. Take another opinion again, for there was nothing to lose, after all, 'and then we'll know where we are', is what he'd said. But the fact was, by then, Elisabeth knew pretty well where she was. By the time she got to Edinburgh last month she knew. And in the couple of weeks that had followed that last, terminal, diagnosis, she'd finished up the Wigmore commission as though lit up from within by a weird excited electricity, wrote it all through in one great piece, the string parts and a whole new instrument line she hadn't even known was there – laid a flute's silvery strand through the entire piece, start to finish, like a silver thread – the electricity that seemed to pass through her own body in the weeks of composition alive in the music itself . . . A trace of her, it might be, like the flight of a bird passing from one end to the other like the flight of a bird through a mead hall – wasn't that how the Norse poem had it? She would set that to music too, if she had the time, that unknown writer's thread of flight . . .

But her work was done by now. And ahead of her: Meeting the conductor. The rehearsals. The performance. That would be the next few, brief weeks of spring. All the birds flown through the music and home and until then she had this flat, these rooms, this piano. So yes. Springtime in London. Magnolia trees. And enough just to be back here, wasn't it? – with one tree right outside her window, by the front door of the flat, the petals of its flowers thick and resilient and curved as wings.

The travel had made her tired though. So after spending those few minutes downstairs, after she'd got in, she pretty much went straight to bed. That's what illness is like, she thought, as she made her way up the stairs. *Is like* . . . It was all absolutely exhausting. She had energy enough to get out the sheets and duvet cover from the linen cupboard, the pillowcases . . . Just enough to half make up the bed – not put the cover on after all, it was too heavy – then when the last cotton pillowcase was on, she kicked off her shoes, dropped her skirt to the floor and crawled into the cool new sheets, drawing up the raw, uncovered duvet close to her, before falling into a dreamless sleep . . . *Is what illness is like.* Was the first thing she thought, hours later it must have been, when she opened her eyes and it was dark.

At first, she couldn't work out where she was at all. She lay there in a sort of state, actually, trying to remember what window it was, what wall was outside the window, trying to remember what it was about herself she had forgotten while she'd been asleep . . . Then there it was again: She was going to die. The remembering itself not nearly as bad as the nearly remembering, those scrambled nanoseconds after sleep when she came into consciousness in a sort of terror, was how it felt. The remembering not nearly as bad as the trying to. More . . . inevitable. Like all of life was. One thing going on to make another thing. One day into another, and some days ending with another day to follow, others just ending.

She lay for a few more moments, savouring the dark and that feeling of coming into rested-ness in this bedroom with which she was so familiar. How many times she'd been here alone in the darkness. Times just like now . . . *Now* . . . She thinks, *Let it be now,* as if she might close her eyes now and the light would be gone from around her. Times like all of those times, early in the evening when she would lay down to rest before going out, taking a few minutes before she rose to get dressed, to get ready, lying quietly and letting the daylight fade slowly from the familiar walls and edges, letting the violet, the shadows in. Or waking in the middle of the night and Ed beside her. All of it, all those times and everything about this room known to her and familiar. All the laying down. All those dusks. Midnights. Sleeps.

In the dark of this particular night, she smiled. It could almost have been one of those evenings from long ago, and she and Ed were on their way out to some big party or there was a concert or a reading he might be giving, a recital . . . That feeling of lying in a soft dark room but very soon you would be stepping out the door and a whole new portion of the evening would open up before you: bright-lit rooms, music, the tap of glasses, chink and rise of conversation . . . In the moment of thinking about it, a whole kind of energy came alive in her in a rush, a feeling of *yes* – and she decided that she would go out. Just go out that second. Put the rest of it off – the phoning, the sorting out the flat, unpacking – and instead step out like she'd stepped out then, single and clear and full of youth and energy and the future. As if nothing could trouble her in the world, nothing at all.

She picked out a pair of jeans from her bag and pulled them on, found her jacket where she'd left it cast across the bedroom chair, and went downstairs and out the door.

The magnolia tree was right where she'd left it. Standing shock still in the night air, the branches whitened in the cast of the streetlamp and all the beautiful blossoms crowded upon the branches but utterly motionless, like each of them was waiting for something. Elisabeth stopped for a second, no, she must have stopped for a full minute, waiting herself as she stood there before the tree. The night was warm. The earlier chill she'd felt in the day, when she'd got off the train, had been absorbed into something lovely in the air, a kind of early summer heat it was like, and the moisture too had evaporated, giving the navy sky and air around her this lovely wide sense of expansiveness, comfort, contentment. She felt as though she could just take off her jacket right there, that she could just be wearing her T-shirt in this dark warm air . . . And she did, she took off her jacket, and with that mood of carelessness came the feeling of being young again, like she was in her early twenties, before composing, before performing, before meeting Edward and marriage and moving to Scotland and to the island . . . Before any of it and here she was, running around the place like she used to run around, going out late, staying up all night and working in bars and restaurants and going to weird, out-of-the-way music festivals and concerts in abandoned warehouses that only started at midnight and were all lit up by candlelight . . . Remember that time . . . *Remember it?* the blossoms asked her. *Who you once were? Who you are?* She realised that when she'd come out the door she'd had no idea what she was going to do with this navy-coloured night but she knew now.

There was a pub on the corner of her street where she used to go, years ago, and she would meet Ed there sometimes, after work, or they would go across for a late-night drink, or sometimes she would go there on her own and take a seat up at the bar, talk to the barman who she knew, and there was an old Irish priest who used to drink there, like a character out of a Graham Greene novel, Ed always said. She would often talk to him too, a clever, clever man, sit for a while and talk with him about sin and death and hopefulness . . . *Where is that old priest now?* The place used to stay open late, she remembers, lying in bed and the window open to the pale blue early summer sky. Not like a pub at all, in London, but like an Irish bar, or a New York City bar. Coming closer to it, though, she saw that it had been painted, given some sort of treatment, a theme of sorts – what was that? It used to be a beaten-up-looking kind of place but now she could see it had been decorated to look that way, that was it, glamorous and tattered, like a kind of salon – still it was the same place as she remembered, the same kind of crowd inside, same kind of music coming from the jukebox, used to be, though tonight it was coming from a band set up in the corner, a guitarist and a drummer and someone on the violin . . . That's who she used to be. *A violinist.* Elisabeth smiled. The door was open so she went inside.

The noise and number of people hit her in a rush. Men and women pushed up around the bar, or were seated at little tables, gathered together and talking, laughing. There was great heat coming off them, energy, as though each person there couldn't be more engaged by those around them, lit up by their company and alive with it, all kinds of people, as though the whole world was there. Elisabeth made her way through them and would order what she always used to order – a vodka and tonic, lots of lemon, lots of ice. It was the drink for parties, remember? The parties? She would buy a pack of cigarettes too, later, and smoke one outside.

'Hi there,' the girl behind the bar shouted a little, over the band. 'What can I get you?' She was Australian, was she? Or from New Zealand? That jolly, capable sort of voice, that outgoing manner. The voice of someone who has spent a lot of time in the sun, lying on a beach beside a big blue sea, on a flat green lawn.

'A V and T, yeah?' she said, when Elisabeth told her what she wanted, and smiled. 'Sounds good to me.'

Elisabeth was fishing in her pocket for money. 'That's it,' she said. 'With a lot of ice, please. And lemon.'

'Like it that way, myself.' The girl smiled at Elisabeth again, only this time held her gaze. 'Everything okay?' she said.

Elisabeth stopped, for a second her heart stopped – was that what was happening? Her heart was stopping? Her body stopping and this was the end, not later at all, as she'd thought, but here now, now . . . Then she steadied herself. 'Can I get change for the cigarette machine?' she said.

The girl had turned back to the drink she was making. 'Nah,' she shook her head, shunting ice into a tall glass. 'Don't have one any more. But I'll give you a fag if you want. I'm having a break in a minute. We can smoke outside.' She turned around and gave Elisabeth another one of her smiles, straight off a beach, full of sun and long hot days.

'Okay?' she said.

'Okay,' Elisabeth replied.

The whole thing just like being young again. That's what Elisabeth thought later. The okay, okay. The no need to worry about anything, about what might happen next, because everything would be okay. That ease, that feeling of the night containing everyone and everyone was there together, that everyone might be your friend.

Okay.

Okay.

She hears herself say the words.

'Okay,' said the girl again. 'I'm going to come and find you, okay, in a minute, and we can go outside together

44

then and do that bad thing.' She made a gesture of putting a cigarette to her mouth, inhaling, exhaling.

Elisabeth nodded, 'Sure', and went back over towards where the band were playing. The violinist was running through a lovely A minor arpeggio, hunched over her instrument like she was an old Highland fiddler and drawing the bow over the strings as if she were at a ceilidh in the hills, that light feathery sound you heard at all the village dances on the island . . . It was pretty, arriving through the thick hum of the bar's chatter and the thrum of the guitarist's chords. And reminding Elisabeth of something. Of her flute, she realised. The flute in her Elegy for Strings, her Adagio – that same quality of an alternative sound that might well not be expected, that did not so much compete with or participate in the music made by the others in the orchestra, but was simply an alternative to it, weaving through the tune and lifting it, lightening it like a flight path of sound cut through the trees. Elisabeth was elated. She realised she was. To be hearing that sound now. And played in this way. And at this time. To be out late at night and on her own, deeply alone, in the way she loved to be, with all the world gathered around her for company if she needed it, but she probably didn't after all. She wanted to dance, and talk to people, to stay out late and . . . stay. The band finished their number and everybody clapped.

'Well,' the singer said. 'Well', and they started into the next number.

A boy beside her leaned in. 'They're good, aren't they?' and Elisabeth turned. He was young. Mid-twenties, late-twenties. Over his head the girl from the bar put up two fingers, mouthed 'Now' and pointed towards the door.

'Are you a musician?' the boy said.

Elisabeth smiled, 'I was.'

She detached herself from him – his hand was on her forearm – and made her way outside.

There was a group of people standing in a clutch, four or five girls in black boots and skinny coats, young men with big jackets and parkas. She took a place beside them, on the corner. From here she could see her flat; she'd switched the lights on before she came out and the windows of the sitting room were yellow squares against the dark air, and light showed too from the bedroom above. The euphoria from before, from inside, was still with her, in her heart, in her head, but suddenly the body felt weak again. She needed to sit down. There was an upturned drinks crate by the wall, a few of them had been put out there as impromptu seating and a number of people were gathered around them, smoking. There was movement beside her, the girl from the bar; Elisabeth took her arm and they sat down together.

'So' the girl said, and there again, Elisabeth could hear, was the sun in her voice and all the blue water. It came from a long, long way away. 'Here we are . . .'

She shook two cigarettes from the packet she was carrying, passed one to Elisabeth and flicked open her lighter.

'You live around here?'

'I used to.'

The tiredness was everywhere, in the bones around her eyes, in her fingertips, in the weight of the paper cigarette she held. She could lay herself down right here, right now, in the street.

'Used to, eh?' the girl said. 'But not any more. Great place to "used to" live,' she said, 'I reckon.' She shook her head, took a drag of her cigarette. 'Yeah, I know that feeling of "used to . . ."'

A great cheer sounded then, the band finishing their set, and clapping and whistling.

'You know . . .' Elisabeth started to say – but couldn't finish. There were the windows of her flat, lit up against the dark.

'I do know, darling,' the girl said. 'I know. The same for all of us, right? The same fucking lovely thing.' She put her head back, her face upturned to the sky, to the moon as though it were the sun and she was letting it warm her and Elisabeth did the same, put her face up that the moon might shine upon her in the same way. Only she couldn't see the moon here, it was London. She'd been alive for a very long time.

'Let's stay here for a bit,' she said, and the girl nodded. 'I'm okay with that. I'm good for ten minutes.'

Ten minutes is all I need, Elisabeth thinks now. And she pointed to her flat, the house, the beautiful tree outside. 'I used to live right there,' she said to the girl, pointing to the lit-up windows, to the white tree, and the elation rushed through her again like a beautiful drug. The rest of it could wait. Everything that was coming. The hospital.

The music. The telephone and the calls and the things she needed to do. Telling Edward that there would be no more tests, that part was over, that she had decided to do this last bit on her own. *Ten minutes.* The flowers were there in the tree, she could see them, each one flocked home for her return. Time yet before they would be fulfilled with the promise of their own blossoming, would fall to the ground and be finished for another year. *Time now*, Elisabeth says to herself, in the bedroom, to the open sky. For now it was as though the same blossoms one by one would detach themselves from the branches and in a great flock would simply fly away.

*

The Scenario

At a dinner party a few weeks ago I saw my old friend Clare Revell and we immediately fell into a conversation about words and feelings. The night before I had watched the film *Melancholia* by Lars Von Trier and I told Clare that I had been irritated by its 'lack of rigour' – is the expression I used, that old line, meaning, in this case, I said to her, the way the film seemed pulled together, affecting as it may have been but pulled together out of many different bits and pieces, using movie stars, particular kinds of characters, film homages and so on, to make it seem important, and all of those moments given gravitas and unity by the same few bars from Wagner's *Tristan and Isolde* – the famous few, at that – played over and over and over again.

'But I don't agree at all,' said Clare – I think that is how the conversation kicked off proper: *I don't agree at all.* 'Why shouldn't a story be made of bits and pieces?' she said. 'And what do you mean by " lack of rigour" anyway? That's just a fancy way of saying someone doesn't do things according to the way you do them, that you don't like their approach. I felt *Melancholia* was a great film, actually—'

'You *felt*?' I said. 'What's the point of you telling me what you *felt*? I want to know what it is about the film that made you have that response – of a "feeling" towards it. I want you to give me a reason why it's great – not just some old "feeling".'

Clare laughed then, showing her gums in that pretty, sexy way that I think Tolstoy used when he drew an image of the little princess in *War and Peace* and describes her in terms of that particular physical configuration, 'she had a short upper lip and showed her teeth very sweetly when she smiled,' he writes. I've always found those kinds of smiles pretty and sexy – surprising somehow – and fun. Blame it on that dear old Russian if you want to. Then Clare took off her jersey and settled into her seat, because this was the discussion beginning fully now; we'd just laid out the opening of things and now we could fully get into the subject and its ideas.

I looked over at my husband in the corner of the room, and then at the other guests. They were all happily talking and engaged. Clearly no one was going to notice or mind if Clare and I got deep into some private, esoteric conversation about feeling and reason that, in a way, didn't belong at a party like this – a cocktail party, really, but with a buffet and music that might lend itself later to dancing – that would shut everyone else out, like a portcullis coming down, 'No Entry', our fancy kind of talk. I had a sip of my wine, and Clare began.

'There's something I want to tell you about,' she said, 'that happened to me years ago when I was still a student. I was reading semantics and philosophy as you know, and it was all Roland Barthes and Irigaray and Deleuze and Guattari. Books like *Language and the Text* – do you know that book?'

I shook my head. I knew of the book but I hadn't read it, and Clare went on to describe it in brief, 'all about signs and the signified' she said, and told me how important it had been to her, that particular title, as a young woman, when she was learning who she was, who she was to be. She'd been thinking about all of this, she said, because she'd just finished reading the new novel by Jeffrey Eugenides, and that book began with a character reading an inspirational book by Barthes, *A Lover's Discourse*. In fact, that information was 'the way in' to Eugenides' novel, she told me, which she had also loved. In fact, she said, she'd even written an email to Jeffrey Eugenides telling him how much she'd enjoyed his latest work, and he'd 'pinged an email straight back', telling her how delighted he was that she'd liked it.

'And all because of a book by Barthes being at the beginning of it,' Clare said. 'Reminding me of a whole period of my life.'

The story, proper – I've used that phrase before, I know – as she started to tell me (we'd both topped up our glasses of wine by now and were fully and cosily settled, like two cats, is how I thought of it, into our chairs – though my husband told me much later that night, before we went to bed, that throughout the entire period of the evening, while we'd all been having those pre-dinner drinks, I'd in fact been sitting in the most vulgar way possible, with my legs wide open so that everyone could see right up my skirt), began all those years ago when Clare was a young woman at the LSE and studying semiotics with a woman who I will call X, who is a leader in her field, the author of seminal texts about meaning and perception, language and the body, 'high, high theory' as Clare put it. 'These were impenetrable books,' she said, 'that I desperately wanted to read and understand because I fancied her rotten.' She stopped for a second, then laughed out loud. 'For me,' she said, 'the books, the reading . . . It was all about sex and love and feelings and wanting her to fancy me and not the world of words, of ideas, at all!' She laughed again, showing her teeth. 'I just wanted to kiss her! Nothing to do with books! And I felt like a fraud because I was supposed to be understanding all this theory and learning from it. Signs and the Signified. I was supposed to be her student and she my tutor – and I felt like a charlatan, an impostor, because really it wasn't about what she was teaching me. It was about bodies and sex.'

'Wow,' I said. She'd given such a clear definition of things. *Writing and the Body* – that was a book I'd read and found very influential at university, myself, by Gabriel Josipovici, and it covered the same kind of ground. 'I see exactly why you're telling me this off the back of what we said about *Melancholia*,' I said. I think I said that then. Because we were having, Clare and I, that particular delicious feeling you sometimes get when talking with someone, about the conversation actually being about several things at once – the primary subject having been about that film, and how it had caused both of us to express quite opposing views, and then this other very different, narratively oriented conversation that had come out of that, all about bodies versus language and what had happened to Clare with a glamorous older woman when she was a student. And what had happened? I was interested, you see, in finding out more on that subject of whether or not the feelings that coursed through any response to anything, whether a film by Lars Von Trier or the story Clare was presenting now, might have value and be of interest.

I was sitting there, as my husband told me later, with my legs wide open and thinking about that – while all the time holding fast to all my ideals about the real artist being someone with a unifying vision, the kind of person, in other words, who wouldn't need to rely on the famous bits from *Tristan and Isolde* – the bits that everybody loves anyhow – to make the audience believe that what had been created was meaningful and somehow righteous, in the aesthetic sense, well made and fit for purpose, beautiful that way.

And there was Clare, just the opposite, who'd told me on a previous occasion that – and she was adamant that she was not being post-modern at all – she always cried in the bit of the film of *Mary Poppins* when the old crippled woman comes out into the twilight and Mary Poppins sings 'Feed the Birds' to her. So yes. We were different, she and I. We were different, all right, and I was intrigued, I was coming to realise, over the course of our discussion, by the rigidity of my own views that seemed so dull, somehow, me sitting there in my black tights and my high heeled black shoes, my short black skirt – what a trip! – next to this free and open-minded intellectual with her pink gums and white teeth and a story to tell . . . That had a river in it, she went on, and a bridge, and the cold air of midwinter on her exposed skin, on her throat and face and, when her shirt was unbuttoned, on her breasts, a story braced with coldness, December in London, a chill wind coming off the Thames, the 'freezing' and 'exciting' qualities of the day.

For there she was in the story, too, wild and free. Fancying the pants off this extraordinary-sounding older woman and – 'What was she like?' I kept asking Clare. 'Like, physically? Tall? Fair?'

'Oh, yeah, all of that,' said Clare, right back. 'She was amazing', and she kept returning to that phrase of how much she fancied her: 'I fancied her rotten,' she repeated.

For that reason, I never got a real portrait of X for the purpose of writing this, something I would have liked, actually, to have been able to create a portrait of that woman in the Henry James way of showing character that is not the Tolstoy way but more uptight and detailing all the moral qualities of a person before you get anything of the physical, like you always get with Tolstoy straight away, the physical, you read about that first. Instead I'm left just with that 'tall' and 'fair' of my own here – enough to make X a Valkyrie, I suppose, to keep the Wagner theme live, more a daughter of the god Wotan than an earthly Isolde – and Clare said she was having classes with this woman every week and loving the classes, of course, just sucking in every single thing about signs and signifiers, and going off and doing all the reading in between, reading that Barthes book and Lacan and Foucault and everyone, and all because she was in love with this person, X, and this was the only way, through reading the books X had read and had written about, those many texts of hers, Clare could get close.

'Finally,' Clare said, 'after all this, after all the tutorials and the flirtation – because I knew she was flirting with me, using the books, her *texts,* to flirt with me – so, finally . . .' And this is what I thought Clare said . . . 'We had a day together.'

Finally we had a day together.

As I say, that is what I thought she said. The next part of the story depends upon me writing it like that – faithfully, but with a sense of drama, of narrative fulfilment – in the way I heard Clare say it, that 'Finally' performing its trick, you see. 'Finally we had a day together.'

Clare knows she looked great that day. She was wearing a leather jacket and a shirt that she loved. 'It was from Flip' – I know I've got that part exact. 'And it was beautiful, beautiful cotton,' she said. When I asked her more details about that later – when we went on to talk about the importance of the feel of the clothes you wear on top of your body, that first layer of clothing and how that makes you feel when you are with someone you fancy, how you remember every detail – she said it was a pale blue shirt with a thin, thin yellow stripe, 'a fine stripe', Clare said, putting her thumb and forefinger together to show how very fine it was. 'It was quite preppy—'

'A Connecticut shirt,' I interpreted. 'Like the boys wear there, on the Eastern Seaboard.'

'Yes,' Clare said. 'And it was made of, as I said, this beautiful cotton and I know I looked great in that shirt. I knew I looked just great.'

So, and again I say it, *finally*, there she was. Dressed as she was – and it was 'illegal'. Clare kept using that word. 'It was illegal,' she said. For them to be having this day together, time out, a whole day, first having lunch, somewhere in Soho and then walking around London, the two of them, in term time, and on their own . . . And they'd ended up on Westminster Bridge kissing – with the air cold, it was freezing on Clare's exposed skin, from where this woman had unbuttoned her shirt right there on the Bridge, had unbuttoned that pale blue and yellow stripe cotton beneath her leather jacket in order to touch her breasts as they kissed. December and a thin cold wind was blowing across the Thames and there they were, these two women, a young woman in a leather jacket and a rather gorgeous sounding boy's shirt and a sophisticated and should I write splendid older woman? (I want her to be splendid, so keep it in), a beautiful tall older woman, her teacher. Yes, 'tall' and 'fair', and they were kissing, they couldn't stop and X had put her hand inside the boy's shirt, 'and she groped me, she was grop-ing me!' Clare said.

She took a handful of the soya nuts she'd been eating and crunched them all down. I saw the flash of those wild and lovely pink gums, those white teeth. She laughed, and I did. We both laughed.

'So you see what I mean?' Clare said. 'It was illegal! For me to be with my teacher this way, for her to be doing that. She was my teacher and I was loving it, kissing her and being kissed, being felt up. I was in love with her, I wanted to run off with her . . . And all of this happening on Westminster Bridge in the cold, in December, we were kissing, it was wild, and then suddenly she pulled back,' Clare said. 'She pulled away from me and asked me, "Do you read *Feminist Review*?"'

'What?' I said. And then, 'Wow.'

'I know,' Clare said. '"Do you read *Feminist Review*?"'

'I don't even know *Feminist Review*,' I said. 'I mean. I've never read it. I've heard of it but—'

'I know,' Clare said again, back to me. 'And I hadn't read it either – but I wasn't going to tell her that . . .'

'So,' I said. 'What did you do?'

'Well I went, *Yeah*,' Clare said. 'I said, "Yeah, a bit. I know *Feminist Review*."'

'And—'

'Then she said to me – and remember the cold air, it was on my face, on my skin, my shirt was still unbut-toned, my jacket was open to the December air—'

'And the river flowing beneath you . . .' I said.

'Sure, the river. And it was cold. It was bloody cold, and a second ago we'd been kissing and she'd been feeling me up, and then – get this, okay? This is the part of the story I've been wanting to get to – she said to me, after I'd said that, yes, I knew *Feminist Review*, she said that, well, could this be a scenario?'

'Hah!' I said.

'I know!' Clare replied.

'Because what does that even mean, right?' I said.

'I thought the same thing! What is that, a scenario?' Clare grabbed another handful of the soya nuts and chewed and crunched and swallowed them so quickly it was as though ravenous hordes were chasing her.

'Well I think it has a capital letter, for a start,' I said. 'But I don't know . . . what it is. Do you know now?'

'I think so,' said Clare. 'But on the other hand, maybe not.'

'Well it's not like saying "Affair", is it?' I answered. 'Though "Affair" most certainly has a capital letter as well. But it's not like that, is it? Scenario?'

'But neither is it just a situation,' Clare added.

'No,' I agreed. 'It's not that. It's not just a situation. It's definitely something that's—'

'A Scenario. Exactly,' Clare said. 'It's what was happening – right there, at that minute. It was her way of saying – what? That this could be the reality for the two of us? To be together? That it could be this big deal—'

'Or also,' I said, 'a way of saying that what was going on was nothing at all.'

'Yeah!' Clare grinned, then she gave out a quick laugh. 'Weird, eh?' she said. 'To use that word when all that time I was feeling so much. You know, the cold, the kissing. My shirt unbuttoned. Feelings you see. It's what we were taking about before. And then this word came down – in the midst of all the feelings—'

'It came between the two of you,' I said.

What I was thinking, that moment, as Clare was crunching nuts and talking about all of this, was that 'Scenario' was a word all right. A word that that glamorous woman had used, knowingly, wisely and slyly, a word she'd used on purpose – whether or not it had come out of the pages of *Feminist Review* – she was using it for her own purpose, that word, to stand, meaningfully and solidly between herself and this young woman she was kissing and fondling. It was a word she carefully, mindfully inserted between herself and Clare, between her hands and the opened shirt, the bare breasts, the cold, shivery skin.

Scenario.

'Like, what is that, right?' Clare said to me.

I was sitting there, my husband said, as I wrote earlier, with my legs akimbo, wide open, like an old lady or a man sits, and I wasn't wearing trousers but a short, short black skirt.

'Scenario,' I said.

'What did it all add up to?' My husband asked me, later that same night. We were having a discussion about the evening; he'd met a really nice couple, he said. He was in television production, but interesting programmes, art and culture, and she was a painter. 'You'd have liked them,' he said. He wanted to invite them for supper sometime.

'I mean,' he said, 'where did your discussion with Clare lead you in the end?'

It was quite late. I was getting ready for bed.

'You sitting there with your legs wide open, like some old man, for Christ's sake,' he said. 'Your legs all over the place . . . Jesus, Mary.'

'It led nowhere at all,' I told him. After all, that wasn't the point of it. We were exploring the concept of language and feeling, the right of one over the other. We didn't have a conclusion to reach.

'Well, I thought it was a bit rude,' my husband said. 'A party, after all, and you two holed up in the corner talking in a way that seemed exclusive. You know, Mary,' he said. 'You two shut all the rest of us out.'

And he was right, when I look back on it. I'd been aware of it at the time, whether it was an okay thing to do, have this separate conversation while the party was going on, I wrote about that earlier, but had ignored the thought.

'She said: *Could this be a scenario?*' Clare said.

An invitation. And a dismissal.

'It was both those things,' I said.

'What?'

'By calling it a scenario,' I told Clare, 'while she was touching you. She was both inviting you to have an affair with her and denying the significance of what was going

60

on at the same time. She was opening up the possibility of something happening, while closing down the likelihood of it ever occurring.'

'Like a discussion about semantics,' Clare said. 'Language and the body.'

'Exactly,' I said. 'The Scenario. It sounds like a short story. I'm going to write it all down.'

'Beginning with this party?' Clare said.

'Oh, don't do that,' my husband told me. 'Don't go turning all that into fiction. Bad enough that it happened, darling. You sitting there flapping your legs around . . . No thought for anyone else in the room.'

That's what he said, I told Clare weeks later, when the party was long over and the story was done. That my husband had said I'd had no thought for anyone else in the room.

'Except me,' Clare said.

'Except you,' I replied. 'The conversation we were having.'

'Was it a scenario then?' my husband had asked me. 'What happened? Did you figure that out at least?' I'd finished telling him about the party, what Clare and I had been talking about. It was late and I was undressing.

'Maybe,' I answered him. I pulled my T-shirt over my head and stood there naked. 'Maybe,' I said again, and then we went to bed.

*

Glenhead

Anyhow she was fed up with him. Sneezing and coughing and pulling out that dark handkerchief that looked as
though it had been balled in his pocket for weeks. It was
revolting. And the children were revolted, her children.
What was she doing with him, anyway? What on earth?

'Mum?'

Some relationships might be okay for a night or two,
an affair, even, for a while . . . But not in a car together,
now. Not this.

'What?'

Not this driving off to look at some house in the
countryside somewhere when she'd promised the children
they would always be city children, that they would always
belong in town.

'I'm hungry.'

'I know,' Sarah said. 'Me, too. We'll stop soon, promise. We'll find somewhere for lunch.'

Because, stability. That's what everyone said children
needed, wasn't it? The importance of keeping some sem-

blance of the same routine, the same life. The sense of the day-to-day having gone on uninterrupted, no matter what happened. You didn't force big changes, not even now, not even after a year had passed. You kept everything calm. Schools. The house. Just have everything stay the same . . .

For the sake of the children.

'Promise?'

Isn't that what everybody said?

'I promise,' Sarah replied. 'Somewhere really nice, with puddings and everything. I promise, darling.'

It is what everybody said.

But who knew, really, what children thought or needed? You just didn't. Like now, with Tim driving and her sitting beside him like a wife. That wasn't anything like routine, was it? Yet, lunch. Being hungry. That seemed to account for most of what the children were thinking now. There was Nicky with his headphones on and Elsa had asked to have some track or other and now they were listening together, Elsa singing quietly along to the song like she was just a little girl.

Trying to drown out, probably, the sound of Tim's ghastly trumpeting and wheezing.

'You really are unwell,' Sarah said, looking out of the window, away from him.

'I know you hate it,' Tim moved his hand, the one without the handkerchief, on to her thigh.

She didn't reply. But neither did she move his hand. She let it sit there, on her leg, like a creature that one feels sorry for.

'Don't worry. I'm feeling better,' Tim said. 'It's a British thing. I swear I never used to get sick at all back in the States.'

Outside, the countryside was flattened into winter, flat brown fields, low brown hills, brown river. The trees were massed in clumps beneath a grey sky and they looked like they were made of nothing more, Sarah thought, than bits of wire, sticking here, sticking there. There'd never be any sap to those branches, no green. Earth formed ridges along the farmland at the side of the road and sheep and cattle stood motionless in the cold. Every now and then a quick brittle wind disturbed the image of it all, the dull landscape, shook it into life. But for the most part nothing moved except her car and Tim driving, coughing, blowing into that handkerchief again.

'I'd say we're about five minutes away . . .' Sarah had the estate agent's details on the dashboard in front of her, and took another quick look at the map on the back of the glossy folder. 'It says here, take the turn off the B768 and follow signs for Glenbank . . . Oh, hang on—'

At that second she saw the sign up ahead.

'It's right there. We're here after all.'

Tim slowed down. There was no sign of any house, though. No gate or any sort of entrance.

'Mum.'

Nicky had flipped out his ear plug and was leaning forward into the front seat.

'This is a total waste of time,' he said.

So there it was again, stability, see? People had talked

about it for months, they still talked about it. That the children were at the age when you had to be careful. No alterations to the day-to-day. No lifestyle shifts.

'A total waste,' Nicky said again.

Sarah could hear the music he was playing buzzing out of the tiny plug dangled around his neck. God knows how loud he'd had it turned up. Elsa was still listening. She had her hand up to her ear holding the little earpiece in place and was mouthing the words now, no longer singing.

Stability. Stability.

'Mum?'

'Can you turn off that thing for a minute, please? I can't hear myself think.' Sarah picked up the glossy brochure, put it down again.

'I don't want to do this either,' said Elsa, her voice without expression. 'I'm still hungry, though,' she said. 'I could still eat.'

Teenagers. They were teenagers, after all. Still, this was awful for them. Sarah knew that. She acknowledged. The whole thing, the car. Tim. Tim driving. Sneezing. Tim himself sitting there next to their mother in the car, the family car. Tim who'd stayed the night the night before, who'd stayed many nights . . . Awful for teenagers, the whole thing. Awful.

'Mum?'

And now here was Tim with her, with them, in the middle of nowhere. An estate agent's brochure on the dashboard . . . They knew something was up. Of course they did. Though she hadn't said a word about the house, about what she and Tim had been discussing, a fresh start, all of that. God no. She'd just said, 'Let's go to the country for lunch', that's all. 'And look, we might see this house on the way.' 'What house?' And she'd shown Elsa the details in the brochure, the big rooms, the stable for a pony. 'But I like our house,' Elsa had said. 'I don't want to move anywhere else.' 'I know, I know. But let's just have a nice drive, okay?'

So yes, it was awful for them. In their own car with their mother's boyfriend driving. Even that word, though Sarah had never used it. 'Boyfriend'. Because that's what everyone said, didn't they? After a divorce and they'd met someone new? No matter how old, people called him a boyfriend. Mostly they did, or 'someone new'.

And Nicky and Elsa had to be with 'someone new', their mother's 'boyfriend' . . . God, Sarah felt ill with it. What was she doing? Yet here they were, in the middle of nowhere, driving off to see a house that they all might . . . What? Live in? Was that really the plan? What on earth was she thinking?'

'It's going to be great,' Tim said. And touched her thigh again. 'Look around us, all. It's beautiful here.'

But was it? Really? On one level. Sarah could see, through Tim's, through an American's eyes . . . The Scottish countryside, all that. Rural Perthshire, and only an hour from Edinburgh . . . Who could say Perthshire wasn't lovely? But now? With its brown hills? In this cold?

'Beautiful,' said Tim again. Though he didn't say 'beautiful'. BeauDiful's what he said. With his American accent. With his cold. Not beautiful at all. Nothing was.

*

They turned off the little road up the private drive. There was still no sign of the actual house. It was like turning into a field, the drive just a swath of dark cut into the earth, through the tall dry sedge that bordered it. In summer all this would be green. In summer . . . Sarah thought. When would that ever be? In summer when all this land around would be cut for hay and golden green? When the trees up ahead, that she could see now, would be in full leaf and casting a lovely purple shade across the lawn that came now fully into view, in front of a large grey house and the glimpse of a river, beside.

'Deserves its name all right!' Tim said, delighted. 'Doesn't it? Look! Behind? That'll be the glen, right? And the river here beside it? Come on—' He'd stopped the car, turned off the engine. 'Let's have a look!'

He reached down at Sarah's feet and pulled up a jacket. 'This will be fun!'

For a second, Sarah had a glimpse of that boyish charm she'd been so attracted to, when was it . . . six months ago? After Alastair had left. This will be fun, he'd said then, too, when they'd met at a cocktail party and he'd invited her there, straightaway, out for supper at some really fancy place. And it had been, fun, hadn't it? Then? When she'd needed some fun? She'd thought so at the time, anyway . . .

Now he walked off away from her, putting on his jacket as he went, opening the gate and leaving it wide, stopping, Sarah saw, to pull the wretched handkerchief out again. Yet he was good looking, wasn't he? Tall, with that American build from playing lots of sport. They all played football, didn't they, American football and it made them tall like that, with those broad shoulders . . . Everyone had said he was good looking. Now he stopped to blow his nose and cast his gaze around the house and its gardens. Master of all he surveyed, is what he would be thinking. Just beauDiful. This damn country. Ah, Scotland. The fishing. The stalking. The life of the gentleman. The whole damn thing.

'Come on!' he shouted back to them. He blew his nose again and gestured to her. 'Come on, you all!'

'I'm not getting out of the car,' Nicky said. Elsa was looking out of the window, away from the house, away from her mother's boyfriend. Nicky had both his earplugs back in and his eyes were closed, his mind full of music.

Neither of them needing her.

Is what Sarah had been telling herself, more and more, these past weeks. Because teenagers . . . What teenagers needed their mothers anyway? And those routines everybody talked about, their mothers' routines? All that stability, where did that get you? Teenagers themselves wouldn't want any part of a routine, they were unstable, that was the whole point of being a teenager. And any moment they'd be grown up and gone and she would be on her own. She would be alone and they would be living somewhere else, and maybe far away. Or, she'd thought, alternatively, as she'd been telling herself, being rational, thinking about the future, she could be with someone. Someone new.

After all, Alastair had been gone for a year now, nothing was going to change, was it? He wasn't coming back.

Suddenly Sarah was exhausted. The weather. The brown, damp earth. Probably coming down with something, Tim's damn cold. Everything felt shivery. Even with the car heater turned on and up and raging away, she wanted to hunch down in her seat, go deep into herself, deep in . . .

Tim had gone. She couldn't see him, he must be around the back. She'd give him a few more minutes and then, okay, she'd get out of the car, she'd go and join him. Have a look around the house like he wanted her to. After all, it was pretty enough. A square Georgian facade giving on to a flat green lawn. Long clear windows. It would be lovely inside. Sarah knew that, without even having to imagine it.

That's why she'd said, 'Why not?' when Tim had shown her the brochure and suggested coming out here. One dead weekend in late January . . . And by now they'd been seeing each other long enough that Nicky and Elsa were used to him, surely?

'You never know,' Tim had said. 'Kids. They love a fresh start like the rest of us. Nicky could have a shed for his drums, Elsa could get a horse if she wants one. I'd buy her a horse.'

So . . .

BeauDiful.

But still they always said, didn't they, the experts? That children needed continuity after divorce? And that women needed to wait, the mothers did, until the flak from the split had settled, before they made any changes? Because the children needed time to come to terms with it, that Daddy's not coming home. They needed time and so everything had to wait until then, until when they'd grown up a little. Stopped believing in happy endings.

Sarah reached in the back for her jacket, rumpled between the two of them, her children, like a soft, soft old blanket.

'Our children,' she and Alastair had said once. She couldn't look at them now.

Quickly, she shoved the jacket on and got out of the car, but then, just for a second, caught Elsa's eye. Just for a second, but it was dead, the look her daughter gave back to her. Like the countryside around her. Nothing was alive there.

'Leave the engine on, mum,' Elsa said. 'So we can have the radio. If you're getting out of the car, I want the radio on. The music we have is too quiet.'

'No it's not,' Sarah said to her. 'I could hear it from the front seat, blaring through your earphones.'

'Well believe me, mother. I couldn't hear a thing. Not with your boyfriend sneezing.'

'He's not my boyfriend. Tim is not a boy.'

'You know what I mean, Sarah.'

'He's sure as hell not my dad,' Nicky said. 'I know that much.'

'Atish-hoo! – Atish-hoo! We all fall down,' Elsa sang.

In a second, Nicky was out of the car and running. He didn't have a jersey on.

'Wait!' Sarah called out to him. 'We can look at the house together!'

'He doesn't want to look at your bloody house,' said Elsa.

Outside, the air was even colder than she'd thought. And damp. She could breathe it, that deep clammy breath of an old, old kind of cold. Sarah was shivering with it. It was in her bones, in her blood it felt like. Christ, she was freezing. So what was going on here? That she would still be holding out here, right now, standing here? Imagining herself in a house she had no intention of living in? Did she? With a man she did not want to be with? With children who looked at her the way Elsa had just looked at her. It was dead everywhere, this place. There was no relief.

Even so, still shivering, her whole body, she walked away from the car with no intention of following her son, she walked around the side of the house and Tim was there, just standing, peering into a window. Not part of any of these thoughts of her own, he was doing nothing. Well, he was blowing his nose.

So – 'We all fall down . . .' Sarah sang the line to herself.

'Shame,' he called out to her when he was finished, the handkerchief back in the pocket of his ugly green parka. 'There's been a cock up with the keys. They're not where the agent said he'd leave them. We can't get in to see the place after all.'

'Oh.'

Sarah was looking in a back window through to a scullery and kitchen. Clearly the house hadn't been lived in for years. There was an old butcher's sink in the room, nothing else. She went to the other window at the same back extension, it gave on to a little hallway. All was dark there. Overall, the house was smaller than she'd thought, than it seemed. The agent's details had it looking quite expansive and when they'd turned into the lawn it was even grand. But not really. Not now that she was close up. It was a bit of a disaster, actually. Like the phrase Tim had just used, that sounded so strange in his American mouth, 'cock up'. That was what this place amounted to, their visit here, her being in the car with someone she didn't love, had never loved, with her children who were her children, her and Alastair's children . . .

'You're right, there's been a cock up,' she said to Tim now. 'It's an awful house. No wonder it's derelict. No wonder it's so cheap.'

'You call this cheap?' Tim said. 'Jesus. I'd like to know what you call expensive. The place is gorgeous, it's got great atmosphere. I looked in the front, there's a staircase goes way up to—'

'Who cares?' Sarah knew she was being mean. 'It just has fake grandeur, that's all. It's not a real house, not for a real family to live in. It's just someone's idea of showing off.'

'What?' Poor Tim. He was all confused. All the sleeping with him, all the talking and discussions. All the letting him stay over, letting him do that more and more. Having

73

him spend weekends, even, getting to know the children, letting him drive her car . . .

'I don't know what you're talking about,' he said. 'Jesus, Sarah.'

'Well, look,' she said to him, he'd started walking away. 'Look at this house,' she said. 'There is no glen to be head of, don't you see? Just a bit of a river . . . It's flat, Tim, there are no hills here, no glens.'

She was talking to herself, really. Tim had left her to it. He was heading back to the car. 'There's no point in staying here,' he called to her over his shoulder. 'We'll have to come back with keys.'

'Don't be silly,' Sarah said. The words formed a frosty breath in front of her face, even though she'd spoken so quietly. They'd never be back. She went around the side of the house, still looking in windows, and then to the front. There, true, Tim had been right, the house seemed to regain itself. There was the dining room, a hall, the interior door open so she could see light from a fanlight cast across the parquet floor, the turn of a banister . . .

'Oh, you're pretty enough,' Sarah said. 'So why are you so alone?'

'Because the man I loved left me,' the house replied. 'He doesn't love me and he's gone away. And I have no heart,' the house whispered, 'only empty rooms, and most of them are cramped and dark.'

Sarah turned away from the window and looked over towards the car. Nicky was standing there by the open back door, Elsa huddled inside. The radio was blaring, awful, awful music with a tinny, electric beat. What were they thinking, her children? Of her? Of this day? Were they thinking about their father, who they loved, or their father's girlfriend who they had met a number of times and now Alastair was talking about them all going on holiday together, him and them together, and his girlfriend, too? Were they thinking about that, about holidays, or only of this, this cold now, where they were, this minute, this brown, brown earth? Only thinking about nothing at all? At her back, the house waited, like her own shadow. Sarah felt its presence, the poor thing. It didn't know either. They were both of them just waiting. Sitting there, with their empty rooms but the door shut tight and locked.

For a second, Sarah wanted to turn and go back. Try to find another way in, break a window. Tell Tim she'd found a loose door back there in the scullery and could he force it. Tell him that they could find a way to get into the ground floor through the cellar, maybe, a separate entrance, somehow, someway, so that she could step into that lovely hall, feel the light from the fan window upon her face, let the house admit her. She would mount the wide stairs then, enter all the rooms and who knows, yes, maybe stay there as Tim had talked about, yes, maybe buy the house and live there and maybe Tim would be her husband and Nicky and Elsa, they would have another father as well as Alastair, and Alastair and his wife, in time, all four of them, all four adults could be here together, in summer, the trees in leaf, the fields green, and they would be having lunch together, all of them here, and the children too, and drinks out on the lawn . . .

But that was crazy. Everything. What was she thinking? The house – it wasn't a real house. She'd seen that already, without needing to turn back to it, to check it again, she knew, the house knew. It was a fake. Where was Tim, anyway? They needed to be getting on.

The children hadn't moved. They were still waiting there by the car, Nicky leaning against it, so tall now, like his father. The music would hold them, Sarah supposed, as long as they wanted it to, they would leave it playing. They were teenagers, after all. What was any of this to them that they should even be thinking about it?

'I promised you both a nice lunch,' Sarah said, when she got close to them.

'Eh?' Nicky looked up, Elsa turned, unhooked the earplug and let it fall, then leaned forward to switch the radio off. The faint but insistent music from the earpiece still sounded in the chill air, a frantic buzzing, like an insect's whirr of wings.

'I promised you,' Sarah said again. 'Come on then.' She touched both of them, her son on the shoulder, her daughter lightly, lightly on the top of her head. 'You two,' she said. 'When Tim gets back, let's get out of here, shall we? Let me find us somewhere nice to go.'

*

STAYING OUT

The Highland Stories

Comprising four separate narratives that are related: Two sisters and their children, two girls and a boy. More information about this family precedes that which is printed here, and follows it, but those stories do not appear in these pages.

The Father

The father said he'd take them down to the beach to go swimming but he never took them. Cassie went into his room three times to see: First time, that he would take them. Second time, to say that they were ready now. Third time, to just remind him that he'd said that he would take them. But all three times the father was asleep.

Seemed all he wanted to do, the father, was stay in that old room and in the dark. Outside it was sunny and Aunt P said they could all get down there to the water on their own. That Bill knew the little sea path over the cliffs, she said, that he could lead the girls safely on their way.

'But the father said he'd take us,' Ailsa said. 'He picked me up in his big arms and he told me and we all believed.' Then she started to cry.

Ailsa was just four though. What would she know? That's what Bill said later, when he and Cassie went down the path alone, their swimming things on underneath their clothes and Bill had a picnic in a bag. 'If you're only four,' said Bill, 'you believe all the lies that grown ups tell. That father of my mother . . .' He swung the bag around and banged it on the grass. 'He just makes up stories. That's what I heard my mum say. Your mum said it too.'

'Did she?' said Cassie. It was like she was wanting to be certain but seeing in her mind already that of course her mum would be agreeing. Laughing, kind of. It was the way her mum and Aunt Pammy were together all the time, laughing and telling secrets like they were in love. *Go away now . . .* That was all her mother ever said when they came up here on holidays. *I need time with my sister, Cass. You'll be the same with Ailsa one day. Your aunt and I have things we need to talk about. Remember? We don't see each other through the year and now's our only chance . . .*

'Yeah,' Cassie said to Bill now. 'I think she did say that. My mum listens to everything your mum says.'

'My mum says the father's stroke-y,' said Bill, heaving the picnic bag from one shoulder to the other. 'That ever since Granny died he's gone funny in the head.' Then he ran down the rest of the hill ahead of her and Cassie saw him on the little beach where Ailsa and the father also should have been, flinging down the bag with the sandwiches and juice and pulling off his clothes in the light and lovely Highland sun.

Cassie loved it coming up here to see Bill and Aunt P. And her mum did and Ailsa and their granny too when she used to visit sometimes and they would all be together and so it was strange having someone else among them, in their private and special world. They never had people who could be fathers here before. *We don't do men . . .* She heard her mother say once, when they were in the village and someone was asking Cassie where her 'daddy' was. Truth tell: She'd never had a daddy nor Bill much either. There'd been daddies once, her mum and Aunty Pammy told them, but that was a long time ago when the children were very little and Ailsa was a tiny baby. Though Bill said he could remember his. Still, Cassie couldn't see a thing when she tried to picture what a father was.

Only here was one suddenly come in among them this summer. Her mum and Aunty Pam's own daddy come all the way over from the West in his funny car. And he used to be married to Granny all the years from when she was a bride and they never knew that too. No one talking about him, thinking about him. Then one day just arriving, driving up the road that afternoon *out of the blue . . .* That was the sentence Cassie kept hearing her mother say. Remembering every time she remembers it with a shock the look on her mother's face when the car came down the little road leading to the house.

Everything felt changed then, from that moment. *Out of the blue.* The way her mother's face changed, that she put her hands up to her mouth when she saw the funny car like to stop herself from screaming . . . Then running inside to find Aunty Pam and them both holding each other like they were little girls and Aunty Pam saying over and over, 'Don't worry, Susan. We're grown ups now. We'll find out what this is all about. Money, probably. We'll give him something and he'll go away.'

But that was at the beginning of the holidays, nearly, and now they were halfway through. And nothing had been found out, had it? And he hadn't gone away? The father just stayed in his room or then in the evening came out and sat, started talking, asking questions like he was waiting for something, a glass in his hand, a bottle on a little table beside him. Bill said the father was an alkie as well as someone with a stroke and that meant he was a strange kind of dad. He'd heard his mum say that, Bill said, when he couldn't get to sleep one night and he'd heard his mum and Cassie's mum whispering in the kitchen after the father had gone to bed.

'He drinks whisky and beer and then he can't talk any more,' said Bill to Cassie, next day, after he'd been up in the middle of the night listening at the door. 'I know everything now,' he said. 'Why he's come. Why my mum and your mum left home when they were little children and never saw him again.'

But what did that mean though, 'everything'? That's what Cassie wanted to know. If Bill knew everything, and the mothers did, then why did everything just stay the same?

In the end no one seemed to know that much at all. Why the father had arrived when they didn't even know their mothers had a father. Why her mum and her aunt should have a daddy of their own and never tell.

When she asked her mum about it her mum just said, 'Shhh. Doesn't matter darling.' She'd be doing dishes or pinning washing out on the line with Aunty P and talking . . . Always those two sisters had so much to say. And the father in his room, pretty much all the time but then he came out in the late afternoon and he started talking too, sitting on the sofa in the sunny sitting room, stretching out his legs like he'd been living there all his life. 'I want around me all my grandchildren,' he'd say then. 'What'll we do tomorrow, eh? Tell me. What would all you little ones like to do?'

So that's how it had come up, that Ailsa had said would he take them swimming, because in the books about families that's the kind of thing the fathers do. They take picnics to the cliffs and they walk down from the cliffs like giants, holding the children's hands and taking bags and tents and things to make fires, all the way to the sea. Helping the children when they fall. Swinging the mighty bags and calling out, 'This way! This way! Follow me!' And the father had said that yes he'd take them. And not just any kind of swimming. That he'd take them out to the rock in the sea where the seals sometimes came, that he'd help them swim all that way, and it would be easy too, he'd show them how to do it, he'd show them the way. 'We'll get a plastic bag for a picnic and I'll strap it to my back,' Cassie remembers to this day him saying. He'd sat there with them all around him, making shapes in the air with his hands, to show them how it would be. What they'd do when they got there, to the beach and the rock and the cold, cold blue . . . All the loveliness of the project gathered there in the patterns shaped in the afternoon sun by his thin white hands, in the dream of them all together for that moment, the sun in the room, the two mothers standing in the doorway like they couldn't quite dare to let themselves enter more fully in but still even they were smiling, they were smiling.

'I'll swim with each of you out on to the rock and we'll stay there all day, make friends with seals and meet a mermaid or two . . . We might even spend the night, build a fire, have a camp . . .'

'And all of that from swimming?' Ailsa said.

'All of that,' the father said. 'Come here, my darling . . .' And that's when he took my sister up into his arms and made her laugh and swung her in the air. It's when we believed.

The Rock

At the end of the garden was a field and we weren't supposed to play there but we did.

Bill said all the kids from his school played there, that they went there in the afternoon, after tea. First they scared the sheep away and then they set up forts and made dangerous games with hideouts and dens that the adults would never know about in that field that finished at the edge and had no fence, because it fell straight down where a fence should have been, straight into the sea.

Aunt Pam said we were never allowed to go there. For the way the grass stopped just like that, like God had cut the earth off the edges and let it drop down on to the rocks with waves that made great crashing sounds against them, making their own storm down there, their own mad and crazy weather.

She had lots of rules about staying on the farm. Rules about gates that you had to close and not bothering the cows when they had their calves with them. Rules about being gentle with the sheep because sheep were gentle, and about how long we three kids could stay out on our own without her having to come looking. She said Bill should know better than to go on about that field and how good it was to play there.

As it was, she said, she was having to phone the farmer every day to tell him that he should get a fence built there again, that everyone should know how dangerous that field was without it. There were certain kinds of winds she knew about, that could just pick you up and blow you away; or other kinds that could push you. Then she gave Bill a certain kind of look and he turned away.

'You should know better,' she said to him. But he still wasn't looking.

Aunt Pam knew about weather and the land all right. Even though it wasn't her farm and she just lived there. Uncle Robbie had been a farmer when he was alive and before Bill became a half orphan then, with no dad of his own. But now she had to phone that other farmer who kept his animals in the fields that she and Bill and Uncle Robbie used to say were theirs. She had to ask his permission for every single thing, as though the three of them had never lived there before with their own sheep and cows to look after. So it was Uncle Robbie told Aunt Pam ages ago, all that stuff about where the north wind came from and what it could do, and he told Bill too – like he knew everything about living up there where they did, about the cliffs and the air and the way there were no trees because the wind had torn them up by their roots, most of them and blown them away.

Bill said that was what came of living in 'the far north'. That anything could happen there.

'You girls won't know about this,' he said to us, wanting to be the one who was in charge when we were up there on holidays. 'You girls won't be aware, but where we live things are different from the rest of Scotland, or Britain even, or England. Because we have things like a dangerous field at the end of our garden, and kids up here know about it – but they're strong. Like I could take you down that field and we could play there, if you're not scared. There's stuff we could do that would be frightening, but exciting too. And if those other kids do it then why shouldn't you? So do you want to? Do you? Do you?'

In the end, I wouldn't know what to say. Aunt Pammy put down the rules but she was busy most of the time, that summer we went up there to stay. She had stuff to do in the house, or people in the village to see. I remember her as a person hanging white sheets on the line, or writing lists for shopping, sweeping the floors and I sometimes think all of it, all the business of her day was just missing Uncle Robbie and not talking about it or wanting to cry. Bill said she wasn't allowed to.

'Never, ever,' he said. That was his rule. Ever since his dad was chucked off his horse at the Highland Show once, he said, and his head cut wide open for everyone to see but he didn't even cry then.

'Because nobody can change that,' Bill said. 'That my dad is dead. So nobody can cry.'

That happened the autumn before though, when Mum took me and Ailsa out of school and we came up to help Aunt Pam and Bill and there was a funeral then and I heard Mum and Aunt Pammy talking and talking, late into the night and it was all about Uncle Robbie and about the farm and something to do with money and how Uncle Robbie had been 'pushed to the edge'. And now it was summer again. And Bill never said anything else about missing his dad or any of the things I'd heard Mum and Aunt Pammy talk about.

'Come on,' he just said instead. 'Tell me you're not scared. Let me take you to the field and we'll do the dangerous game.'

So Ailsa and I said we would, that yes we would go.

Disobey Aunt Pammy and be irresponsible, for that's what we'd be, she'd told us, that it would be irresponsible and sly to disobey any of the rules of the farm. But still we went with Bill one afternoon when she was gone from the house and it wasn't sunny that day, but it was warm and grey and there was no wind to push us.

'Stay with me, girls,' said Bill. 'I'll look after you.'

The game it turned out was no kind of game at all. The minute we got to the field I realised all the time Bill had been lying. About games going on there. About the kids in his class going to play after school. There was no game. We walked out across the grass, going deeper and deeper into the field in the still grey air, and there was nothing about us, nothing. I felt how still it was and quiet, and how in the distance the sheep moved away from us as they saw us coming, looking up and seeing us, staying for a minute and then moving away, making that sound, the lambs did, like a baby crying.

'Come on,' said Bill. 'This is what we do' – and he led us further and further across the field. Everything by now was getting slower. More distant. The house was at our back and the low slate garden wall and the air was soft and warm and grey and everything had stopped except our walking, getting further and further away, walking across the field and knowing at the edge there was nothing. High up I could hear the curlews sweeping and calling their sad cry but Bill wasn't talking and Ailsa never said anything much, she just followed me mostly and understood without having to say things – so when

I knew there was no game and that Bill was making it all up, the game of playing in the field, I could guess that Ailsa might know it too, that Bill was doing something altogether different here.

I watched him up ahead. He had a stick and he was waving it in the air, at first just walking across the field but then I saw he was getting closer to the sheep. He was waving the stick and then he started waving it at the sheep, and they started moving faster, scattering away faster from him and frightened, running, and I knew that it was all wrong.

When Aunt Pammy said there were rules at the farm she also said she'd learned them all from Bill's dad like she learned about the weather and the other things and Bill knew the rules too in the same way that his father had taught him. So Bill must have known that if his dad had stayed alive he would never have let Bill go out there the way he did that day. He was a man who probably would have put up a fence himself there to protect the sheep from danger, to keep them safely in. He would not have let a boy go running off towards the edge of a field that dropped straight down into the sea. But he was not there. And the farm had never been his, my mum said later – a lot of unhappiness in that family, and broken hopes, for the way Bill's dad never managed to own property for himself and work a piece of land. Maybe it was that pushed Bill's dad 'to the edge' – that sentence I'd heard my mum and Aunt Pammy say, as I stood at the door listening in, that worries about money and the farm they couldn't manage had driven that man to such unhappiness, that I thought when I heard about it, that of course that would be a reason that he would just have to die.

I think I thought that, anyway. Actually, I can't remember properly in what order I learned about any of these things. Even now writing about that summer, and remembering it or the holidays before . . . It seems a long time ago. And we don't go up north any more, and we don't see our cousin and our Aunty because now they've moved far, far away.

But that day with Bill doesn't seem in the distance. Seems like just now Ailsa came up behind me and took my hand, not saying anything but frightened for the way he was being with the poor sheep. Chasing them and screaming at them and waving his big stick. I started going faster, trying to catch up with him then but I could feel the way the field was running out under my feet and I couldn't make myself go faster because of that, the way the field was disappearing into sky as we got closer and Bill was chasing one of the sheep closer to the edge.

'Stop it!' I must have shouted. 'Please come back!'

'Please come back!' Ailsa said as well because she was only four then and when she did speak she always had to copy.

'You can't stop me, it's the game!' Bill turned and faced us. We were close to him now and his eyes were glittering, his cheeks bright red from running and yelling. He was breathing hard in and out. 'Just watch!' he said. 'Just watch what I can do. Here—'

And he turned back then and for the last few steps ran the sheep ahead of him, it letting out that little baby sound and scattering its woolly tail and running on ahead from Bill's big stick and his frightening cries.

'Watch!' he yelled again and in that second the sheep went over. One minute running on the grass, the next it was gone.

'You see?' Bill shouted at us. 'You see what I have done? And how dangerous is the game? Look—' and he grabbed my hand and pulled me and Ailsa closer, closer to the edge.

We were two steps away and I was sick to look down but I had to. Down the drop to the swirling sea and the big black rock jutting out. And way down there, split open with red stuff coming out of its white wool, the poor sheep he'd frightened over. Its head twisted queer off to one side, and the legs all sticking out in different ways.

I felt something swirl, like the sea that was spinning around the big rock and then Ailsa let out a scream.

'Cry Baby!' Bill yelled at her then, and pushed at her so she screamed again. 'Cry Baby!' he shouted at her over and over and at me too but he was the one who had tears all down his face, not us.

'That's where my dad went,' he shouted, 'so why shouldn't some old sheep get killed down there too? If I want to I'll make them all go over! The whole bloody lot of them, all the people! My mum and your mum and all the whole families in the world. They can all go down there to the rock!' He was crying, and he was banging his stick down and down, into the ground.

'I saw him,' he said. 'When he didn't think I was looking. But I saw him go down on to that rock that's down there with blood on it . . . And now it's only fair that all of you should see too!' He was shouting and crying and banging his big stick but we were away from the edge now and Aunt Pammy was coming running up behind to pull us all away and back into the field even though he was still shouting and crying . . . Even when she took him in her arms, shouting into the soft and warm grey air that felt like heaven with no sun at all and the rest of the sheep gone quiet now in the field behind us, but as Aunt Pammy held him closer and closer, tight in her arms, and tighter, little boy, not shouting any more but only crying by then, 'I saw him and it's not fair, it isn't,' he was saying to her, just to her in the end, as she held him close, 'that it was only me.'

Dirtybed

My cousin Bill loved animals but he killed them too. It was part of living on a farm, he said. You loved the pets and kept them but then you got rid of them just as easy. Like the little Easter lamb and we put a daisy chain on its head but Bill's dad stuck his knife into its throat just the same, and Bill put all the grey kittens that Ailsa and I had been feeding right into one big potato sack and dropped them in the river, in the deep part, beside the waterfall and they'd never be able to climb out.

This all went on those summers we used to go up to the farm. There'd be a little creature, a rabbit in a box or those sweet kittens, say, and then they weren't there any more. In the same way Bill's father, I suppose, was there one summer but not the next. It was just country living and country life – is what my mother thought about it. Even though she didn't know that much to say. She was only a person who lived in the city and she had her job there and it was me and Ailsa that knew farm things because of Bill and Aunt Pammy and Uncle Robbie before he was gone. And so my mum and Aunt Pammy were sisters? They were pretty different, they really were. My mum wouldn't do the things Aunt Pammy did.

The animals stopped being killed after Bill's dad was gone though, even if Bill kept on the habit with the knives and the stones but by then there were no more baby calves or sheep to look after, no more chickens or geese. He helped Aunt Pammy get the heads off the last of the hens, I saw him do that in the first week we were there. And the dogs that weren't working any more . . . Neddy who used to help Bill's dad with the farm shot them all, one by one, and Bill wanted to help him do that too but it wasn't the same as the killing before when Uncle Robbie had been around. Those dogs weren't like the other kinds of animals anyway because Bill's dad had kept them, he'd let them live. And they'd had puppies that grew up and worked on the farm too or else Bill's dad sold them or gave them away. But now all of them were also just dead. Neddy took them into the barn one after the other and in the end Bill couldn't use the big rifle because he was too young. 'Besides,' Neddy said to us kids, 'it would break my heart for Robbie's boy to do it. Like it breaks my own to have to.'

Neddy had to get a job in town then, because the farm got taken back by another farmer and there was nothing for him to do there after the shooting of the dogs. Still, I thought things seemed a bit the same for a while, even with Bill's dad gone and the animals not there. After all, Ailsa and me were on holiday there, I suppose, like every other year, is what I thought then, and that was the same, and it was the same fields around us and the sea at the bottom of the cliffs and the house was the same.

But something had changed after all. To do with Uncle Robbie not being there – but not in the way of him not walking in the door any more, or missing the things he did or said. It was more because there was no more mess like there had been mess when he'd been living there, with the blood and bits of killing. No more of him going around the house with his boots and with the mud, bringing inside all that stuff he used to do when he was out amongst the farm, in the cold paddocks by the sea, or up in the hills on his own.

And Aunt Pammy seemed in a way quite happy, I thought, I noticed it, I mean, after Uncle Robbie was gone, that the man she was married to was no longer there

94

to bring mess in that way. The house had no great boots in it, sitting in the hall, or guns, or knives on the bench and with bits of animal stuck to them, or gutted fish in the sink in the scullery . . . Instead Aunt Pammy put flowers in vases and there were clean, empty rooms. And other things too, like there was one little puppy left from the litter after the mother had been shot who was allowed to come into the house and Aunt Pammy made up a bed for the puppy, in the kitchen where it was warm, and I saw her sometimes leaning down to pat it and talk to in a soft and gentle way.

'Mum's getting fancy,' is all Bill said, when I asked him what he thought about any of this. It was because he was a boy, maybe, and become a half orphan because he no longer had a dad. And so Aunt Pammy turned into this person who wore dresses sometimes and I saw her put on lipstick too, and scent, and she went out of the house without telling any of us what she was doing, just went out into those big summer nights when it never got dark . . . Maybe that was hard for him to see.

Oh Bill, I don't know what you were thinking. In your bedroom with all your toys piled up, those boxes of your cars and farm things and your clothes and your drawings, and you slept in there at night with the door closed when before, when you were little, you kept it open for Uncle Robbie to come in, wearing his farm socks he'd had on that day and the old jersey he always wore. He used to sit on your bed and say goodnight and the door was open then, into the hall. But now it stayed closed. So perhaps you just couldn't see, like I saw, like maybe only a girl

might see, though my sister was too young in those days
to notice . . .

But the killing from before seemed truly gone. And not
only the smearings from blood . . . But the knowledge of
it, the dark part of the farm Uncle Robbie always brought
in with him, that he sat with his son with, to say goodnight. Now there was only a boy left and a father who was
not there. And I thought Aunt Pammy would be sad that
Uncle Robbie was gone and that the farm was no longer
theirs and that the animals weren't there – but instead
she let the little puppy play in the house and there was a
kitten too, from the cat who lived in the toolshed, and she
didn't make Bill take it away and its brothers and sisters
and put them in a sack.

Instead she let things in. She let them come in,
allowed them – is a word she might say – in the way
Uncle Robbie hadn't allowed things before on the farm.
For now it was a house, not Uncle Robbie's farm any
more and when I saw her again drawing on that lipstick
in the mirror one night and then smiling at herself, at
her refection in the glass . . . I knew then what Bill in
his room with all his things around him might never
know. Even with the house all tidy and the door wide
open into the summer night. Even if I was to tell him
myself what I'd seen down at the beach while he lay in
his room, with the door closed, and his father's jersey
with him in the dark.

But would I tell him? Ever? That the man who was
around the village that summer, a visitor from town

Bill reckoned, who had been down on the beach a lot of times, just sitting on a rock or walking around, flicking stones into the water, came over to me that night, after I'd followed Aunt Pammy out the open door, gone out of the house myself, and asked me, 'Have you seen your aunt?' and I looked behind me and she was right there. With her pretty dress and her bare brown arms and her hair let long, and smiling in that same way I'd seen her smiling in the mirror so I ran away then, without answering him or even saying hello, back up the hill and fast, back to Bill but not saying a word to him even then, though I might have, because in the end there was something in the house that might have been familiar to him after all.

That if you had looked, Bill, if you had been able, you would have seen too – and that it was nothing like the house tidy and the floors all swept and bare. And nothing like the scent and lipstick in Aunt Pammy's room – but that her bed when you opened it up and looked inside was dark with something, dirt I thought, like from down their bodies and on their legs from them being together like I'd seen when I turned at the top of the hill that day and went back down the beach and they were there, your mother and that man. Then you might have understood as well, perhaps, if I had been there in the bedroom with you to show, that what she had been doing, your mother, out in the open nights, in all that wide air, bringing it back into her bed and leaving it there through her white sheets . . . Was a mess like another kind of killing. But if you never asked me where your mother was those nights when your father had gone . . . If you never asked, then I would never need to tell.

Ghost

My sister Ailsa didn't talk much. She didn't want to. It was because she listened instead, and she watched. She saw things and she noticed but she didn't have to say, 'I saw.' She kept it in.

This was during those summers when we used to go up to the Highlands to stay with our cousin Bill and my sister was still only a little girl. She followed around after me then, whatever I was doing, and she copied Bill too, always just wanting to do the same things. Go out in the fields, say, to look for baby rabbits but we never caught one. Or make up a secret picnic using the cakes Aunty Pam had just baked and we'd find the place Bill said he used to go to with his dad, when they used to go deer hunting, when his dad was alive and he took a gun.

They'd be away for days at a time then, Bill said. He always told so many stories about his father. How his father showed him how to camp out in the hills and stay the night there by a tree where it was sheltered. How they would build a fire and pitch a tent and sleep until morning, his father getting up when it was dark to let off a shot with the rifle, scare anyone away who might come close. He was making all of it up, of course.

I say that now – 'of course' – but that's because I have always been the oldest. Older than Bill even though he acted so grown up and six years older than my sister who, as I said before, was always just a little girl. And 'of course' I write, because I know now that my cousin was telling stories, but also knew, I think, back then, that stories were maybe all he had. So thinking of them as lies then? Something far from truth? I can't answer that, remembering. Sort of, I suppose, is what I could say. Some part of me understanding that Bill could have never spent time with Uncle Robbie in that way, that Uncle Robbie had died before he could have taken Bill anywhere, done any of the kinds of things Bill talked about – but another part of me swallowing the stories too and being the one who was believing. It was who I was, those summers. The kind of cousin who said 'Yes' when Bill asked me if I believed him. Saying 'I believe you' when he told me that his father was killed by a murderer, a mean farmer who used knives on him or poison or a rope. Or that someone else had pushed his dad, and robbed him first, then lied about it because he was jealous. Because his father was much too strong and clever, Bill said, for anyone to dare to be his friend. Did I believe that? In that father of his who had loved him best? 'Yes,' I said. Always, to everything, 'Yes. Yes. Yes.'

And Ailsa, she just watched and listened. With Bill's dad dead, well and truly, driven off the edge of the cliff down on to the rock one night when it was late only none of the adults talked about it. So it was Bill's stories we were left with, and nothing like the real one, that his father was a failure and lost his money and couldn't care for his family at all . . . Only these other stories instead, that got bigger and more exciting and the stories changed. With the poison, say. Or a strangling. Or saying that the motorbike his father rode was racing, not his own, and someone fixed it, like in James Bond, or some other film, so it lost control. Or how Bill and his dad were out late one night and a helicopter came down and took his father away.

So my sister listened and she didn't say much. When Bill told her about him and Uncle Robbie getting lost in the snow sometime and Aunt Pam had to send out the whole village to look for them. Or about Bill's dad being charged by a stag so he had to wrestle with it, bring it down on to the ground and its antlers had sliced up his arms all the way down to the bone.

'What do you think about that, girls, eh?' Bill asked. 'What do you think about me and my dad being so tough and strong?'

'I think it's good,' I said.

But Ailsa just looked at him, she didn't reply.

Thinking about this now, writing it down . . . I can see those stories of my cousin must have started long before this particular summer I'm talking about here. For years we had those holidays, in that house where Aunt Pam and Bill and Uncle Robbie used to live, way up in the top of Scotland. Every July we went up there, my sister and I, while our mother had to stay in town and work.

So we were used to it . . . We were used to Bill's stories. That place, you see, that farm where my cousin lived, was so known to us, the house and paddocks and the hills . . . Everything about it . . . was familiar. Even when it changed and the house felt different and the farm too because the farm was taken away from Bill's family and it didn't belong to them any more, it turned out – though that's another story and not one to tell here – it never had.

For sure there was no longer the same feeling of being able to play all over the fields like we used to – with the animals gone, and the land was going to be used by some other man for his own farm and his own family. So that then we had more time inside. And maybe thinking more. Making up other, different games. And after a while there was Aunt Pammy starting to pack up all their things in boxes, the house already half empty, she and Bill getting ready to move away. 'From memories,' Aunt Pammy said to me. 'I can talk to you girls about this,' she said. 'But I can't tell Bill.' She was tucking us in at night and Bill was already in his room with the door closed. Aunt Pammy was sitting on my bed and I could smell her lovely scent, the thin cotton feel of the pretty dress she was wearing. 'It's hard for Bill to be here without his dad,' she said to Ailsa and me. 'It's why we have to leave. You girls understand that in a way my little boy can't.'

Even then, Ailsa didn't say a thing but she nodded then. She did understand. More than Bill who was nearly ten. 'It's because', she said to me, 'they have to leave his ghost.'

That is what she said. Those words. And when my sister spoke you noticed it, you listened, because, as I said, when I started this story here, my sister, well . . . Mostly she kept her thoughts right in. This night, though, when it was late and after Aunty Pam had been in and said goodnight and then she'd gone out of the room and I was just lying in bed and through the window I could see the outline of the hills against the sky that was a sort of green so it wasn't dark at all, not really, but trying to get dark is what the dark was like in those long high summer nights up north in those days, long ago . . . Just trying . . . Ailsa sat up in bed and told me what she'd seen.

The ghost of Bill's dad, she said. He was in the house.

'He's in the old bedroom,' Ailsa said. It was scary. The room where Auntie Pam and Uncle Robbie used to sleep. 'He's in there and Bill knows about it. He's been in there and he's seen him too.' She was sitting up on her bed in her white nightdress and with her blond hair sticking up like a little bad fairy. Something about her strange and queer, something in her seen a scary thing.

'The ghost's in there now,' she whispered. 'I could show you. Sometimes he goes into Bill's room. I can hear him in there too.'

All this . . . I'm saying. Writing it down. Out of her silence, suddenly there were my sister's words. Knowing these things. Telling them. How the ghost had always been in there, and that's how Bill knew the stories. Because the ghost had always told him what to say, his father always told him. That ghost had been with Bill for just about as long as Bill remembered, she said, telling him things, talking about adventures, giving him instructions. So Ailsa had been listening around the place, and seeing, understanding somehow something I dared not believe in, though I knew, too, that she could not be lying – so . . . I asked her would she show me, take me there and I could see him for myself, that man who'd once been married to my mother's sister, was father to her child, though no one had ever seemed to know him at all. I knew I couldn't sleep then, not possibly even close my eyes, until I could prove to myself something about this, find out about this thing though I was scared and it was like I couldn't swallow and my heart had got big in me and full up like I wanted to tell someone else, a grown up, but there was no one around to tell.

So quietly we got up, Ailsa and I. She held my hand and went ahead into the dark that was not dark but was quiet and full of shadows and that darkest green. It was like Ailsa was the big sister and I was just the one who would follow. Even so, through we went to Aunt Pam and Uncle Robbie's old room where they used to sleep together once, maybe, in the big old bed that belonged to Uncle Robbie's mother and then she gave it to Aunt Pam as a present on her wedding day. There in the room it was, that same great big bed, with the matching set around it, the chest of drawers and the cabinet and the big old wardrobe in the corner and the door of it a bit open. And it moved.

Ailsa gripped my hand. 'There!' she whispered, and pointed. The door seemed to open a bit more, creaked, and inside the wardrobe, sure enough, I saw a man's form, the old tweed shape of a man called Uncle Robbie. He was standing there with his back to us and murmuring something, he was speaking the low words a ghost has to say.

The light was deepening in the room, from green to grey as though the room itself may as well have been a coffin, with the window darkening and only open the tiniest bit to let in some air, but everything dusty and closed in and silent – apart from that creaking wardrobe door moving just a bit and the thing inside it talking to itself, Uncle Robbie's tweed suit that he was wearing.

'Shhh,' Ailsa said to it. 'Shhh. We're not here to hurt you.'

The suit may have been his favourite suit. It might have been the suit he wore on those days when he was still a father, those days that I could not remember. When he'd been a husband and he had a farm and he lived there with his wife, my mother's sister, and her little boy. Before he went off on his own and before he went off and left them for good, driving himself off over the edge of the cliff at the bottom of the paddock and everyone knew he did it himself, on purpose, that was the story that was true . . . Before any of that, there was the suit that Uncle Robbie used to wear on sale days or when he went out with the other men, the farmers, to go to the Agricultural Fair and the Highland Show, the thick tweed suit he was wearing now to come back and visit us all.

'That's him,' Ailsa whispered, and just then I remember the feeling exactly – it was like a spell that was cracked. *That's him.* In the second of those words I took a step towards the wardrobe so I could see . . . *Him.*

And not Uncle Robbie at all. Not who he was. Just his suit hanging, that's what was there. Just hanging cloth and thick and tweed and warm but no body in it to wear it. No man. No ghost. I went closer, and closer, right up to it, to touch it. To put my arms through. And as Ailsa stayed behind at the edge of the room – even as I touched the suit, for I did touch him, what was left of my uncle – I felt for myself how thin he was and not there, how there was nothing there.

Yet still the murmuring sound went on. Though I had by now my arms among the empty arms, the jacket against me like a chest that was collapsed and flapping, that had never had a body or a heart inside . . . Still I could hear a murmuring on. Secrets. Stories. What I thought had been the ghost's quiet talking to itself, my uncle telling all his secrets out, about why he'd left his family in the way he did, his own child . . . All his secrets . . . All his talking quietly in the grey, darkening room, just a low hum, of talking, murmuring, just the sound of him was all that was left of him, of Uncle Robbie, of his awful, lying ghost . . .

I knew then that it was coming from my cousin's room. The voice was there. Bill in there, in his own bed with his dad's old jersey that he'd taken in with him like he did every night since he was a little boy, to sleep with him. And it was Bill talking to his dad I could hear – making up the stories he would tell Ailsa and me the next day, and fill the air with them, fill the day. 'My dad said' and 'My dad and I' and 'My dad told me' and 'My dad is going to' . . . All of the words to fill the space, to make the stories real, whispering them out on his own in the night that by now was going green no more and into grey but into dark.

'See?' Ailsa whispered to me now, as I went over to her, where she stood at the doorway, but I was a big sister again, taking her hand and leading her back to our room. Passing the closed door of Bill's bedroom and hearing his low voice coming from behind it.

'See?' Ailsa said again, as we passed his door, and her hand tightened on mine.

'Shhh.' I was the one who told her now. Not wanting her to speak. For enough of speaking. Enough of words. Of stories and of lies. Of saying someone was a hero when he'd killed himself, not died at all those other ways, like in a film, but did it himself, because that's what he most wanted, what he chose, to plan it for himself to be that way, leave his family, be alone. Leave them without him on their own.

'Shhh,' I said again – but not to quieten her. Because in a way Ailsa had not made it up at all, about Uncle Robbie and what she had seen. It was true. What she'd thought. What she knew. That he was like a ghost exactly in that house, that man. The clothes still hanging there but empty. Only the jersey, like a body brought down, in a little boy's bed.

*

The Caravan

Was parked up. Right there on a lay-by off the old north–
south highway, the far western side of the country. And
O but it was cold there. The seas were big. Turquoise in
colour in winter – with the eleven days of this story taking
place in winter and this was the eleventh day.

And the caravan not so old but it looked abandoned.
By which I mean: 'Quite broken'. Rusted, well, not rusted,
maybe, but with an appearance of rust. A *semblance*. All
that salt water, you might say. All that cold weather coming in off the sea. The window had been knocked through
by a stone and the door banged half on and off its hinge
whenever the wind blew, and yes, the wind blew. Inside
the caravan it was dark and wrecked and damp with cold.
There was broken glass, a bit of sodden cloth on the table,
some playing cards. This was, remember, the eleventh day.

On the tenth day the caravan stood next to a calm sea.
There on the lay-by, beneath a pale blue winter sky. The
gravel upon which it was sited was wet, gutted in places

with puddles. The caravan on its blocks as though it had been there for years, for years it looked like. *Years?* Yes, as I say, it looked like that. A semblance of years, for sure. A 'permanent fixture on the landscape' one might describe it – one who lived in this part of the country, who knew its lonely roads and the beaches no one visited and the sea in which no one swam. 'That caravan has been there for as long as I can remember,' that person might say. O really? O yes. For as long as I can know.

For the caravan – it has no wheels, only those four cinder blocks – so it's not going anywhere. A holiday home then, once it had been. A place to go to beside the sea. White, with a crimson strip – but it wasn't new. The unexpected sun shone on the chrome of its broken window, the surround of its flimsy door. That was on the tenth day.

The day before had seen a large storm. O large! Terrifying! O the waves were like walls! For there is nothing like them, those storms they get over there on the west, those old west coast storms! O nothing!

And the caravan just shuddered, had to. Just bore the storm out. Bore the weather, remember? Coming in through the window? In through the half-open door? It was *as though* years passed. While the rain came down. While the wind battered at the roof. The playing cards blew about crazily, crazily inside. The Jack of Spades. Ace. A Red Seven. They flipped and turned. On the ninth day.

*

The eighth day was also windy. But not the same as the day before, for this day it was as though the wind were only practising, turning. It was only getting started. The boulders sat on the beach, they sat there. And the great logs that had been washed in from who-knows-where, how faraway . . . They lay there too, like waiting, while on the beach the wind practised, whistled up and down the pebble shore.

Wheee! Like the sound of all the years passing.

Not that there was anyone to hear it, remember. O no. Just the caravan. On the eighth day. With something inside it, rattling.

Because on the seventh day an animal had got in. Through the broken window, or it came through the door when the door had been pulled wide open in a sudden gust. It ran across the floor and up the front of a cupboard. Some food had been scattered on the floor, on the bench, by the weather, by the wind, quite scattered. And maybe that had been what brought the animal in, had got it started. And O you wouldn't have believed it – the brand names of that food! On the packets! Quite fancy? O yes! Tiny delicatessen crackers and pre-packed cheeses. Some silvery foreign tins. All this removed from a cardboard box in a small old fashioned caravan. On a lay-by, remember. In a place you can barely imagine in your mind less go out on a real road and see it. Cry: *Look!* As though you might cry. For this is an abandoned caravan and yet here are wrappers saying Fortnum & Mason, Zabar's, Ladurree.

Be careful the papers don't blow outside, get airborne and come to float on that cold enormous sea.

On the seventh day.

'Be careful'

Is what she might have said to him, when he suggested they go there again.

'Be careful we might end up there,' she might have said. Parked up for ever by the cold and frozen sea. 'Be careful that if we go there,' she might have whispered, 'to our caravan, we might never leave.'

And now it's the sixth day and in the middle of the night the rain started, it fell. And the cloth, remember? On the table? It collected water like a bandage collects water. The tablecloth drawing water to it so that other parts might be dry.

O! O! O! the woman might have said, if she had seen it. 'My tablecloth! Spoilt!' And all for nothing – for damp is in the place, nevertheless. *Nevertheless.* And it's wet and it's cold here. And it's midnight. And there is no moon. And the sound of the rain on the gravel, on the caravan roof . . . It falls. It continues to fall.

The day before was the fifth day and another of the almighty storms, wind now, all wind. The poor curtain fluttered at the window, ripped. There was nothing any-one could do. The cards were lifted from their places on the table. One here, lifted. One there. A whole pack of cards but nevertheless all of them are scattered. Fluttering in numbers upon the floor across the bench, the table. Ace. Jack. Red.

That was the day the door came off its hinge and wouldn't sit square again to close. And O the noise it might make! Banging! *Screeching!* That thin, thin tin!

When the wind stopped, the day before, a seagull came to rest on the roof of the caravan. It seemed blown on to the roof of the caravan from across the sea. The sunlight played across its white feathers, caught the gold in its eye.

They used to enjoy looking at birds, the man and the woman. It was something they used to do, together sitting at the small table. Hearing a great screeching through the window of the caravan as great packs of gulls wheeled and landed on the beach and on the water.

O! O!

Making sounds that were like crying.

Calling to each other, over and over, through the cold air.

Now there was only one bird. Looking out to the sea to where it had come from. Perhaps. Hoping to catch a glimpse of another. *Perhaps.* That it might call to it as the others had called.

That it might be heard.

And the third day was a day for crying. The day the boys came, put a stone through the glass. When they forced the door of the caravan and went right in. Unpacking the food from the boxes, exclaiming at the fancy papers of the packets of food.

Not a day at all but late on the night of the third day, this. After drinking in the pub in town. There was beer and then tequila and then getting in the car and driving fast, with broken lights, down that lonely road beside the sea. The youngest boy, perhaps, the one who saw the caravan as they flew straight past, who noticed it, *caught sight*, and said to the others, 'Stop! Go back!' and they did: Backing up hard into the lay-by and piling out of the car. Approaching the caravan. Breaking the glass. Reaching in to take the lock off, push through, force open the little door. O yeah! They say. O wow! O check this out! They push and press against the little walls. One unwraps a pretty chocolate, eats it. One pisses in the corner before leaving.

Yet on the second day all had been so tidy in the little home. *Complete*. The curtains drawn. The door shut firm and locked against – against . . . All kinds of unpredicted weather. Snow on the mountains inland. Cold off the southern sea.

O be safe, little house. Be firm.

Sitting there, bright, in the frost, in the early morning. Of the second day.

Like you may sit there for ever.

Waiting for them to come back to you again.

For that is what they loved to do, the man and the woman whose caravan it was. They loved, more than anything, used to love, to return to that place. Return. Re-enter together the little door. And wasn't that first day just the kind of day that was perfect to come back to? The reason people keep caravans in the first place, keep little cabins by the sea? So to have a window on to all that sky? So to have a high winter sun, and enough heat in it, in the middle of the day, to remember summer?

'O yes . . .' he'd said to her smiling, drawing her gently out of the passenger seat of the car and into the wide air. 'O yes, you see? You remember, what it's like here? What it's like for us to be here?'

For it is a caravan, after all. It's just the place to sit in. 'A caravan we've always loved. Where we can be at rest, my dear. Remember? How we love it here?' So taking her, this very gently, by the hand and leading her, leading her . . . Towards the caravan door.

And, again, 'You see, my love?' he says again. 'You see? How gentle it can be here? You and I together? This place we love? That you remember? You remember . . . See?'

But didn't see, himself, and could never have predicted it – that the moment his back was turned, after putting her inside, seating her at the table with the pretty cloth that she had once stitched for him, for the caravan itself, its tiny table, and hemmed, and embroidered . . . Could not have seen it nor predicted . . . As he went out to the car for the cardboard box of special foods, for the chocolates from Fortnum's that she loved, or the caviar from Zabar's that he spread for her on toast – that as he brought the world out for her to that lonely place, she would be gone . . .

Run off towards the sea like she's a swimmer! O! Like it's summer and she's running to the sea – O –

No!

Like she's swimming and it's summer –

No!

And this some kind of other, very different sea.

So he drops the box, and starts towards her, out the caravan and down the empty beach – but she's run so far away from him by now, in the seconds, moments, that he left her, that it's like he'll never catch her, that he'd spend his life in trying – for she's running into air is what it's like, that she would be the cold wind herself and all the cold air . . .

O!

O!

Whistling, empty. Down the pebbly shore. Of the empty sea.

But he does. He manages to get there. To where she is in the water, wading in so her skirts and her coat is sodden, he pulls her away . . .

And the story finishes – or begins – there, with the man and the woman at the edge of the sea, at a beach where no one visits, on the western side of the country . . . And the sound of the wind – O! – and the draw of the cold waves on the pebbly shore the only other sound . . . And the man puts his wife back in the car and he drives her away.

The day before that with nothing in it. Nor the day before. Nor the day before.

Only, O . . .
and the draw of the pebbles on the lonely beach . . .
O . . .
O . . .
O . . .
O . . .

*

Foxes

I was coming down the hill and I saw them, how close they were around me. At first, not seeing them, for there were only trees and leaves and paths of shadow, but then making out from amongst the darkening branches small delicate shapes that were moving in between the thickets of elm and oak and ash, taking form and particularity that was animal.

I look back now, on that moment, of something becoming apparent to me in the gathering darkness and it doesn't seem to be evening at all but rather a time of growing light. As though, as the colour left the summer sky and as I criss-crossed my way down the hill, lost and confused and unable, I thought, to find my way out of the wood, I was actually coming into some kind of illumination, an understanding. *I see* . . . I remember thinking quite clearly as the foxes darted before me on the path and then came to stand, like ghosts or children all around me: *I see*.

For sure it was that time of day when anything could happen.

*

I'd been up in the park at the top of the hill, the one with the high black and gold railings around it and two ornate gates through which you enter and leave. The grass there is kept clipped close as a carpet, and in the middle of the green is set the beautiful gold bandstand like a crown. We'd been watching an open-air opera, sitting there on the grass with the singers before us slipping in and out of and around the ornate iron pillars like they were creating a sort of dance. One lover passing to the next, the music like ribbons winding around them, binding them to their story of desire and inevitability, their fate: Don Giovanni and his loves. Don Giovanni and his way down to hell. It was a perfect early summer's evening, high and blue and golden as though it could never get dark, and lovely, I think it was. To be out on the grass with this fili-greed piece putting itself together on the stage in front of us – the singers with their brightly painted faces and their feathers, and the tiny silvery orchestra with its flutes and violins playing off to one side. As I say, it was love-ly, I think. It looked lovely, I mean. Being there in that park Andrew used to take me to all the time, up above the woods . . . Sitting on the shining grass with Andrew and his friends, champagne in our long-stemmed glasses . . . It may have looked like I belonged there. Like I had a place amongst that group of young men and women I seemed to be a part of then. 'Friends,' I might have called them, only they were Andrew's friends – turning to each other and whispering, with a sense of intimacy, collective knowledge, bound together as the singers were bound to the music that wove around them and drew them to the stage . . .

'Isn't the soprano there on the right just like that girl you used to go out with?' somebody said. Turning to Andrew, then looking at me.

'Don't be mean,' someone else whispered. 'She was awful, that girl. None of us liked her. '

'Don't whisper,' another whispered herself. 'We're supposed to be watching.'

'Yes but we're talking about what's-her-name, that girl Andrew used to love.'

Words like that, you see, close up, knowing words. 'How can you talk that way,' I said to them. 'In front of me . . .' Like I knew them well, had been friends with Andrew's friends for such a long, long time when really I hadn't known Andrew for more than six months but still he and those people he knew . . . They had gathered me in. So, intimacy – yes, it is the right word for the group of us brought together on our picnic rugs, sipping our champagne. It even looks like a word that could have whispered in my ear that night and had me believe in it, put its arms around me and hold me for ever.

For it was the night Andrew had decided that we were to tell our friends that he and I were going to get married, that he'd asked me and that I had said yes. It was like a beautiful secret that had been between us for the past few days, he'd said, this knowledge of what he wanted us to do, but now it was time to announce it to these people that he loved – before his parents knew, or anyone in his family.

Before they could 'get to it' as was Andrew's phrase. For his family were like that, Andrew was always describing them. The kind of family who could 'get to things', change them, enter in. The kind who made decisions and spoke in loud voices and did what they had to do when they wanted to do it. The kind of family that made me feel I could never say a single word.

'My mother will want to get to it,' Andrew had said to me and I'd laughed and kissed him then, though the feeling I had was like a little wrench, a twist somewhere deep inside me where you were, my love, where you were first beginning. If I'd known myself at all I would have stepped away from him that moment, Andrew, poor Andrew . . . But I didn't know. All I had for certain was the knowledge of this other secret, the one Andrew didn't know about, uncurling itself cell by cell inside me in the dark. And even as I reached up to kiss him and felt the wrench I knew for certain, too, that this other secret was the one I mustn't tell.

In the meantime there was this plan, he and I together in the park, the friends, the picnic rug. All laid out beneath the golden bandstand on the grass. There would be champagne, champagne, then down the hill and back to the flat for supper and Andrew would make the announcement about our wedding and wouldn't everyone, wouldn't everyone just love to come . . .

And I was to leave early, that was part of the same plan. To go on ahead, make way, prepare . . . As Andrew had said I should go ahead to get everything ready and that's what I'd fully intended, in my usual frightened way, to run quickly home, taking the shortcut path Andrew and I knew so well, be back at the flat in time to get the barbecue on and the salads and dishes arranged, more champagne and an ice bucket and the glasses on the table for when they all got back and Andrew would say, 'We have a surprise announcement to make!' So down I went through the wood. Leaving them all to the part just before the Don reads out his list of lovers and begins his descent to hell. Taking no more than ten minutes, I thought, ten minutes to get down the little path through the trees, down on to the street and back up our road, to be there before the rest of them, the table laid outside and perfect in candlelight when Andrew and his friends arrived.

But the time was not, after all, the summer afternoon I thought would go on for ever. It was later than I thought, and the light was nearly gone from the sky when I was halfway down the hill and I lost my way. Somehow I had taken a wrong turn, and then another, and now I was confused, disorientated, running faster and faster this way and that way but getting nowhere, following one path after the next and terrified, terrified of where I might be . . .

When I became aware of that movement in the trees ahead, a flickering like shadows but then I saw it was the foxes crossing my path, and as I slowed down they too seemed to still themselves, stepping away from the growing shadows then and coming towards me, delicate and wild, not frightened at all.

And when you grow up I'm going to tell you this story. Of how you came to be. And why we live the way we do, you and I, set apart and with our own secrets, in our own world and no one knows about us really, and they may never know. For by the time I had gone through the wood that night everything had changed. *I see* . . . And there would be no wedding announcement. No champagne toast. No visit to a clinic as there most surely would have been a certain visit to a clinic, for Andrew's mother would 'get to it', before her only son's wedding would ever be allowed, would have got to you, for sure, my love . . .

For there was something about those slips of form in the twilight changed things, made of blood and bone, their steady eyes upon me, but as though they were magic, faerie . . . When of course it was me who was not real. I understand that now. Running down through the trees when I thought I knew the way, in that place between the road and the park that kept such wildness in, that meant I was lost, for a time I was lost with nowhere to go but in the end found out I was not lost at all.

Because, of course, I never told. I kept you safe. Inside like a secret and the foxes showing me the way, finally down through the wood. So when I got to the street again, the twilight had worked its spell. Taking me from day to peaceful dark and I was running up the street to pack a bag to leave in minutes the house, the life I thought I was going to step into as surely as one of the players on that park stage had taken their steps through Mozart's score. Becoming instead like a fox myself, slipping out of everything that was known and planned and calculated, disappearing into leaves and trees and you and I, darling, we're gone.

*

NEVER COMING HOME

The Wolf on the Road

Twenty minutes in, the sky started lifting. The thick, grey pelt of early morning cloud was pulling apart, exposing a kind of light that was pale as the shell of egg or dry bleached bone. All day it would be cold. Anna knew it by the colour, colourlessness, rather, of the sky. She knew from the moment she could see the dawn appearing that it would never be blue or sunlit or golden but only the thin cold stillness you got in this part of the country, this season. Only white or bone or grey.

She feels now, looking back, that the sky itself was like a premonition, the colour of the winter light. She had no idea what she was doing. To be out there alone as she was that hour and Neil and the boys asleep back at the hotel . . . It just describes the person she was then, she thinks now, that she would be acting as though by instinct, with no symmetry of reason or awareness. She can't even remember what her thoughts were that morning, if she'd had any thoughts. Noting the sky, sure, and driving that red rental car like it was her own, with the same kind of inevitable feeling she had when she drove at home, that she knew the way to all the places she needed to go . . . She remembers that. And that word: Inevitable. As though being out that morning and her certainty with directions, with her plan, was just like she was driving to the supermarket or dropping the kids off at school. Following turns in the road as though they were familiar, as though every exit and signpost were known to her when really everything she was doing that morning was unaccounted for and new.

Was that what it was like to be in the midst of an affair? To be pulled along with no consideration of consequences, acting as if by rote, as part of a routine? Did all women feel that way? Like the woman in Kate Chopin's *The Awakening*, remember? Or that film she'd watched last year on TV when Isabelle Huppert had run off and left her husband behind in Paris? Was that what it was always like? The feeling of leaving – that you would simply get up in the morning and go?

Inevitable really did seem to be the word for it. Like a word you could hold in your mouth like a piece of food. Like 'edible'. 'Inevitable'. In a way, the same kind of word. A word that wasn't quite finished, even so, that left itself whole inside your mouth after you'd finished saying it, the last syllable sitting against your palate like an object and making you aware, somehow, of the length and loll of your tongue. She says it again, out loud. 'Inevitable.' A word that stays with you. Long after you'd left your sons and husband and your life with them behind.

That morning, certainly, it had been as though she'd had no choice. The destination fixed, the route already planned. *Just get up and go* – that really is how it had seemed. The hotel had still been closed up for the night when she'd walked out the front door, the lights in the lobby bright but no one on the desk to see her. And all the ski posters up there on the walls, and the leaflets on the low tables – 'Snowy Mountain Chairlift'. 'Hilltop Ride'. Like they were reminding the hotel guests why they'd chosen to stay there. 'Best snow of the season right now,' someone on reception had said when they'd been checking in. 'You've come, absolutely, you've come at the right time.'

The sky had folded back some more, as she was driving, lifted some more. Anna had looked at her watch. Seven forty-five. So an hour had passed behind her. Already a whole hour since leaving that bright lobby, and before that, being up in the dark and noting the time then on the bedside clock before gathering up her things, a little bag, a coat, the car keys, and slipping out the door . . .

'Just think of time in pieces,' he'd said, hadn't he? Robert had said. 'One hour. Another hour. Then call me from the box at the end of the road like I told you.'

The sound of his voice comes back at her now, as she remembers all this, the slow drowsiness of it, but insistent. It pulls at her still. There was the road, running smoothly alongside her, with his voice in it, and the seconds, minutes passing like the awareness of breath. Even the car had seemed to have a kind of an animal draw to it, all muscle and speed, like it was running alongside the road with her, keeping pace, breath for breath, second for second . . . Seeming to run the road down with its own strong sense of destination and need.

'Call me at nine,' Robert had said, 'and we'll sort something out.'

That had been the night before, of course, when they'd made that plan. When, as they'd arranged, she'd phoned from the hotel to work out how they were going to see each other, what they were going to do. 'We'll sort something out' had been his phrase the night when they'd first met as well. 'You'll have to call me from the box at the end of my road because you won't get reception on your mobile,' he'd said to her. 'But not too early, okay? I'll be sleeping.'

Had there been something, Anna wonders these years later, in Robert's manner right there at the beginning, when they'd first met, that in its very carelessness was fixed to draw her in? For it's possible to see, isn't it, from her perspective now that she's older, that he may not have expected that she would follow through the way she did? Because for her part, she'd done exactly what they'd talked about that night in London when they'd met. She'd left Neil and the boys eating spaghetti in the hotel restaurant, their faces burned and happy from the day's snow and sun, said, 'Hold on for a sec, I just need to get a cardigan from our room', and had gone instead to the telephone by the bar and called him just as he'd said she should, that they could find a way to meet the next day. Yet there'd been a feeling even then, that she'd barely dared register at the time, that he seemed bemused, perhaps, or even a little surprised, that she would have actually got in touch.

'It's too much now for me to take this in,' he'd said to her down the phone. 'I thought you were skiing. I thought you were . . .' He'd paused, or so it seemed to Anna, '. . . with your husband.'

'I was,' Anna had said. 'I am, but—'

'Shhh. Don't worry,' he'd said then. 'We'll do as we said. But just make sure you don't call me before nine. I like to sleep, remember? I won't be ready for you before then.'

'Okay,' Anna had said. She'd felt like a child.

'Okay.'

Then she'd gone back to the table and Davey looked up and said, 'Where's your cardigan? I thought you were getting a cardigan, Mum,' but the other two were still twirling pasta round their forks, having a race to see who could be fastest, and didn't seem to notice she'd been gone.

So that's how she'd come down off those hills that day, where she'd been with her sons and husband, a day a long time ago, come down off the hills – may as well call them 'The Inevitables'. Because it's a good name, isn't it, Anna thinks now, for a place where a story might start and where it might go to, where it might end. She and Neil had always loved it there. Since way back, before they were married, and then afterwards, from when the boys had been able to walk and they'd got them up each winter . . . They loved that part of the country, and even better that they could get some skiing in over the early part of the year. As the boys had got older it had become a sort of ritual. Staying in the same hotel she and Neil had discovered, taking the same room with the little balcony that overlooked the tree-tops and the long drive that wound down from the hotel to the road. They used to stand there and smoke cigarettes together after they'd got the boys off to sleep, they'd have a whisky or two and it used to feel fun, like their own special game, coming to this place no one else seemed to want to come to, when everyone said skiing was so much better in France or Italy . . . It was the feeling, with the boys tucked up in bed, that they'd only just started going out and that this was their first year together and they didn't even have children yet or a house with a mortgage and bills and arrangements and endless lists of things to do . . .

So when did it stop being fun and just become routine, another routine? When did it happen that anything in her life that was given, like a gift, instead just seemed to cause a kind of hunger, a wild ravenous feeling inside her that nothing was enough, nothing?

So yes, Anna thinks now. Call the hills 'The Inevit-ables'. Make them part of the story, too.

For the feeling had only got stronger. And perhaps had always been there, from the beginning, before she was married even, and just lay sleeping . . . But then sud-denly it seemed the boys were seven and nine and they weren't little babies any more and she couldn't pretend they needed her and relied on her in the way they used to. And Neil – well, Neil was Neil. And she'd known from the moment they first met that he would be a man who would be dependable and safe but in that same way would go deeper and deeper into himself as he got older, the comforts of work and home and family satisfying to him and fulfilling and just that, just comfort.

So no wonder then . . . She can see it so clearly . . . No wonder that when she'd met Robert that night, at a New Year's party when it was cold outside and snowing, and made her think of being up north, up in the hills . . . She'd be ready to run.

Hello, you, he'd said, across the table from her, before they'd even been introduced. *Where have you come from?*

Anna smiles now, thinking about it. Because, really. What a line. Unbelievable, it seems, that she would have fallen for that. Because no one made those sort of comments any more, once everyone started getting married. But, there, Robert had looked at her, spoken, and suddenly at the dinner party that night it was as though all the years fell away of contracts and partnership and children and safe, safe houses, like in a second he brought her up close to herself and she felt open to the world and vivid and alive. Ten years of marriage fallen off her like a heavy winter coat and now she could run free.

And yet . . .

Anna thinks about this a lot these days . . . Ten years is not such a long time, really. To find a life not enough, the choices that you made not enough. To feel distant from a husband, discover that two people don't really know each other much any more, or have that much that wasn't about the children they've had together to say. Ten years not that long at all. For you need way more than ten years to discover that it's not the big, long things that you choose, like a husband or having babies, that show you who you are, but it's the moments in your life, the sightings. That's how she thinks now. And that although the moment of meeting some particular man at a dinner party was no doubt the beginning of the journey she made that winter morning, when this story opens, and that though, no doubt, she'd felt all those things about her marriage back then – entrapment, boredom, worse . . . Really, she knows, it's not the journey, length of time of a marriage, the road . . . But the thing that springs out at you makes you swerve, be alert, turn the corner, that's the real.

Yet there she was that morning all those years ago, even so, and it felt like the act of escape sure enough, back then, to be leaving. All the things that she had wanted, that she had *wanted* . . . She has the image still of Neil lying there in the hotel bedroom, unknowing in the dark. The two beautiful sleeping boys. She'd looked at them and not even kissed them goodbye. As though they meant nothing to her, she'd just slipped out the door, like through a gap in the fence. Choosing Robert. Driving to him. Choosing him, this man she didn't even know, over everything that was familiar. Just catching his eye at a dinner one night, then the two of them starting to talk . . . And the rise of herself within herself . . . Chaos. Is what it was. She remembers strongly even now the charge of that feeling. The wonder of it. The way she couldn't see anyone else in the room then, hear anyone else. Poor Neil down the end of the table and instead this other man close to her, his eyes holding her eyes, and him saying, 'Well I know exactly where those hills of yours are, where you and your family go skiing. From what you tell me, I'm very near. I have a house right there.'

'Really?' she'd said to him, looking steadily into his eyes. 'You know where I am?'

'Sweetheart, I've been going there my entire life.'

She'd smiled. 'I don't believe you.'

'If you want me to prove it,' he'd said then, 'come and see for yourself. Your hills from my gate. I'll be staying in my house at the end of this month. You said you'll be there then. You can come to me.'

Which is when the affair started, she could say afterwards. Or, at least, the literal beginning of the affair. The way he'd made it into a kind of bet, that she would end up being in the car that morning. Following the line, the road . . . One hour. Then another hour. Just like Robert had said. Time in separate pieces. All choices come down to this – no choice. *Inevitable.* So that even when she'd called him from the hotel lobby, and then later, much, much later from her mobile out in the corridor and his voice had been thick with sleep and he'd not known who she was, this woman calling him in the middle of the night, 'What? Who?' he'd said . . . Still, all that inevitable too.

'Give me a minute,' he'd said.

And she had. She'd stood in her knickers and T-shirt out in the hallway, the rest of the hotel asleep, her own husband and little boys oblivious, and she'd waited. For him to wake up. Remember who she was. Already imagining, as she was standing there, shivering, the going towards him, the road being devoured under the wheels of the car and the miles closing in with each second, closing the distance between her and him, imagining – what his house would be like, when she went inside it with him, into his house, into his hallway, his bedroom, into his dark open bed.

So, sure, that morning, all she'd wanted was to get there. It was nearly nine o'clock, and any minute she would be pulling off from the main route and going down the exit, following the slip road for a few miles before there was a turning and she took it and there ahead of her would be the telephone box Robert had told her about, that marked the end of his drive, sitting out in the middle of nowhere like it was waiting for her.

The car pulled beneath her, a loping, easy feeling but hungry, too. The trees flicked past, the miles ahead empty and the sky-lifting hills, the snow and her family at her back . . . There'd been no other traffic on the road at all that morning, had there? Maybe earlier, while it was dark, but not now . . . She swept around a corner and saw something up ahead.

It had taken a second or two to register, another, and then, as she got closer, at the speed she was driving, she saw it was an animal, wounded? It was leaping and twisting in the middle of the road. As the car rushed past she caught the look in its eye – then swerved, veering suddenly, dangerously out of the lane and off towards the verge, regained, and saw in her rear view mirror that it wasn't wounded, there was no blood, but something else had it leaping from one side of the central reservation to the other, across the concrete boundary and back.

What was it, the animal? Something terrified, something wrong with it to make it twist and turn like that. Was it wounded, after all? Injured, and in pain? And only a matter of time before some other car behind her going to come upon it, bring it down . . .

Anna's own car ran on. For what else could she do? Later, she thought about that a lot. What else could she have done? A main highway after all, the charge of speed at her back, and you could only go in one direction, couldn't stop, couldn't slow down even – but still there'd been the feeling of being held, for a second, in an eternity of time, by the look in the animal's eye, its yellow, yellow eye, that just for a split second had focused on her as she'd swept past . . .

That feeling comes back on her now.

For as she'd rushed past, with her own heart jumped up at her with the shock of swerving, and the shock of what she'd seen and even so driving on and away, Anna had taken in, at some point, hadn't she, that there'd been a group of houses, impoverished little new builds, with tiny yards that led out on to the back of the motorway with poor excuses for windbreaks or sound-breaks put up to protect them from the road, and she had understood then that that's where it must have got out from, from that cramped little place in which it had been, no doubt, illegally kept . . .

And was out now, out there on the road. Not knowing what it was doing, how it had got there, where it would go . . .

That look in its eye . . .

But still, what could she do?

The thing that springs out at you makes you swerve, be alert to yourself, turn the corner . . .

She'd kept going. Saw it getting smaller, smaller in her rear vision mirror. Still twisting, leaping. Back and forth, back and forth. The car picked up speed again and she drove on, and for a few minutes even then did nothing . . . Then she slowed down, reached for her phone, putting in the redial number without taking her eyes off the road and miraculously got reception, a clear line.

'Where are you?'

And everything had changed by then. When she replied, answered him.

When she said, 'Just . . .' and heard herself speaking the word. For what was in that 'Just'? Just . . . Nothing? That it was only a word, only an answer for him because she had no other language for him then, to describe what had happened.

'Anna?'

'Just . . .'

Or was it that in that one word she came back to words, while the road went by, the trees flicking past . . . That all she'd needed was just the space to answer him. A word, a 'just' . . . Before she could speak to her husband again.

Whatever it was, before he said, 'Well come back, for goodness' sake', it was like the present had become the past and everything that had brought her to that moment, every thought and feeling, gone.

And she could answer him fully then, 'I know, I am. I'm on my way.'

And see? How the rest of it, like the story that's already run, becomes fixed now, how all of this part becomes inevitable like the part that went before? How Neil told her that he would call the police, that she needed to tell him exactly where she was as they would have patrols out and would have someone in the vicinity who could help. That people did it all the time, he said, kept these things as pets and sometimes they escaped, trying to get back, he supposed, to the hills in which they'd once, long ago, in another lifetime, belonged. He told her to take the next exit and get back on the main road headed the other way, that they could be by the second chairlift at eleven, that the boys would be pleased, that they'd been asking at breakfast where she was.

'What were you thinking?' he said. 'Heading off like that? Without telling us?'

'I don't know what I was thinking,' she'd replied.

Which was the truth. 'She had no idea what she was doing', remember? The story began that way. Through the morning. Through the night before. The beginning of her leaving, the idea she had of breaking with them all . . . The whole passage of time commandeered by feelings that were strange to her, unknown. The only certainty, the thing she knows now with a jolt of clearest sense, is that when the car turned the corner that morning and swept past what she'd seen on the road, caught the look of, in its eye, before leaving it forever twisting and turning in her rear vision mirror all those years ago . . . Was the moment when she herself had broken free.

*

Tangi

The tiniest fronds we called newborn. They were bright green and damp, growing up close to each other on the bank and smaller than my little finger, curled up with secrets at their tips though their stems were nearly see-through in the bright summer light. Newborn, see? Not at all bunched up and hard like the big old *ponga* ferns that grew brown quickly and crackled, straight out of my Nanni's earth. Just 'newborn', her word for them. 'Little babies, still wet in their creases . . . Feel . . .' she said, and she showed me how to poke my fingers into the nub of the leaf, feel the stickiness there that would make the plant grow.

I learned everything from my Nanni then. Before growing up, before getting old. My parents took study leave most summers when I was a child, from the university they taught in, and I'd be sent up north every year to my mother's mother's house. And long those days were, filled with idleness and hot weather, swimming in the river at the bottom of Nanni's garden or sitting out on her front veranda, watching the freight train pass by across the far paddocks, going down through the middle of the country all the way to the sea. And wild. It all was. Even that train, going off into distance. As the house in its garden was, with its ferns and the tangled bush in the back gully, hiding its river like a cool secret . . . So different from where I lived in the city with my parents through the rest of the year. For Nanni's was dark and the rooms in angles, is my memory. There were her bowls of messy flowers on the tables and in the kitchen dishes draining on the board, something cooking on the tops. It struck me like the heat every year I arrived, the great change between the two places I knew as 'home'. And for the different places, different words. Like 'newborn' for a leaf, like 'come here you skinny and let your old Nanni just eat you'. Different kinds of speaking for different lives, those half sentences of hers with laughs in them that didn't even finish sometimes, or went into a question. Or the way words got turned into something my Nanni went ahead and did. Her saying just, 'Who loves you best?' before picking me up and holding me right in next to her, so I could feel her big body like pillows. 'Who's got you now but your old *Puki,* eh?'

She had someone else she loved though, not only me. 'My Lovely Lady' is what she called her, Queenie: 'My dearest, sweetest friend'. She was someone just as old as my old Nanni and so known to her they may as well be sisters, they both told me, 'underneath the skin'. Queenie lived

in the country, out on the *marae* with her family on land
they'd always had there – only she came in. Once a week.
Or twice. Sometimes more than that I think she came – it
all depended on the lorry her cousin Pete was driving and
whether he had to deliver vegetables or pick up goods in
town.

'Pete coming?' I would hear my grandmother say, down
the black phone in the hallway where she stood talking to
Queenie most days. And then I heard laughing, and whispering into the big mouthpiece like she was just a little
girl. 'Oh yeah?' she might answer then and with other
ways of talking that my mother really hated. 'I'm seeing
you then tomorrow, you.' Or, 'Get yourself in here like I
say so, hear me? You move your big behind!' All sentences
like that with nothing in them of the special manners that
my parents so believed in. I don't think they could have
realised back then, my parents, how much I heard, how I
stood witness to this language through those summers in
the way I did. If they had they would have surely stopped
my visits all those years when I was small. My mother
hating it, if she had known, that Queenie came in.

But she did come though, and she did stay. All that talk
down the phone between her and Nanni just a plan for
the two of them to get together for as long as they could,
drink their cups of tea and sit out on the back step like
they would always have more things to say. Sometimes
Queenie might be there the whole day and then we had
our supper, big tea, we called it, outside too, Pete getting
in late after he'd been at the pub and I'd hear the lorry

idling out on the road in the hot night. No manners then either with him yelling for them from out there and hooting the horn. 'Time to wind up, you two talking women, hey? I'm getting up the road so come on, old *Wahine*! Shift yourself, old girl!'

Queenie was *Wahine* all right. She was full *Maori* and seemed not one bit of her 'gone over' – that was my Nanni's expression for her, for her lovely dark. Not one fleck of white was in her, not a single crazy granny or daddy gone off with a *pakeha*, not one. 'She's full, honey,' Nanni said. 'My Lady. She's complete.' She was *Ngarawhahia*, come from twenty miles out from town and twenty miles a long way in those days on twisty rutted roads that snaked through the yellow hills and back into the native forest behind them. It was like a story to me, to hear about what it was like out there. Nanni and Queenie would sit talking, for hours, it seemed, about the family that lived together with all the babies and the nannies and everyone they knew and it really was like a story, to hear the lovely long names of those people and about their Meeting House that was carved all over and dark inside where they might sleep sometimes, and the place by the kitchens where they dug the *hangi* in, to cook the big lunches and feasts. Even the lorry Pete drove described it, covered thick with dust from the roads and maybe a dog or two dogs on the back, jiggling around with all the leftover vegetables that he sold in town . . . Like it had been driven out of another place and time and parked up there in front of Nanni's. Come straight out of another world.

But Queenie, well. If all this was a story then she was the main character here. And just waiting for me to remember her is what waiting to write down any of this has been like. The way her laugh was louder than any other person I'd ever heard, her face closer. The way she wore men's jumpers with holes in them over her summer dress, gumboots or bare feet, depending on the weather. How she didn't care for clothings, that's what she called them, or sitting quietly because why should she when she had so much to say? And what would be the point of that, anyhow? Of quietness? There'd be enough of quietness, she always said, when she was dead – and going on for ever too. 'Awful bloody quiet here,' she sometimes called out to us when she'd just got in, Nanni and me sitting in the kitchen and not even the radio on, no other talking. 'Gives me the willies, girl,' she'd say. 'Come on and let's get the billie on for tea.'

All this of course like nothing my mother would have ever said or done. And Nanni kept it from my mother too, the way she was with her dear friend. How changed it was in Nanni's house those times when my mother brought me up at the beginning of summer and came to fetch me again at the end . . . Because those afternoons, those mornings . . . Before she drove away again in her smart car . . . Awful bloody quiet then, for sure. My grandmother had a part to play, I see now, and acted it, during those brief visits, behaved just like my mother then who never swore or raised her voice or played with words in any of those other ways I knew about from Queenie and Nanni when they were together. Like Nanni herself was different when my mother was around. No 'eh' then, or laughing or the *te-henga Maori*. No little jokes or half words, phrases, that might come in. My mother always said that questions should be proper invitations, see? To dialogue and not just crowded in. There were rules about things like that, she said, and not to be broken. 'Please' and 'Thank you' and keeping your sentences whole. 'Finish what you start to say,' she said. 'Have phrases that, from the outset, you know will contain within them just the right amount of words for all that you intend to show and to convey.'

Aueee. Poor girl. My mother. Hope she doesn't read this now. For the minute she was out the door and gone my Nanni pulled me to her, and held me in, sang one of the old songs you don't need a mother for, just ancestors, just all the dead. We closed our eyes, both of us, to allow my grandmother's daughter time to drive away, get down the road, then *Aueee*, Nani said, like lamenting, like a sigh. Half words and lines creeping in again slowly, slowly as the hushed air took form around us, the silence and relief now that we were on our own. 'Hold on to you, you little,' Nanni said as she squeezed me, ground her teeth. Then she scrunched up her nose to make a funny face. 'Who's got you, eh? And always keep you safe. Let's call our Lady now, you and me. Let's get her in.'

Is how it always went, when my mother was gone. First her visit and the strange ways, then the sound of the car driving away, Nanni getting Queenie on the phone and everything all right again, her back with us next day, or the next, and they talked about it sometimes, my mother's mother and her dear best friend. And sometimes, too, they would also cry. It's where that kind of talking would lead, Nanni told me later. It's where it was bound to go. Those days, as the hours went on and their voices got low and the tea sat cold in the pot, the slops in the cups, Nanni would turn away from me and talk so low to her Lovely Lady that I could never hear, was not allowed to. 'Run away,' she'd say then. 'Your big old ears don't need to listen. Go!' And I knew it would turn into sadness, when she set me apart from her that way. The stories they told then always made my Nanni cry.

As I say, my parents can't have known that this was going on. Queenie coming over and the tears, and I always kept it from them easy, the talking and the things I came to learn. Looking back now, I think how my mother must have dreaded those years that I would surely find out sometime just the answer to the secret that she tried so hard to hide. But then, all of us, my grandmother included, were of a family so well used to behaving the way we did that it could only ever be *just-keep-it-in-girl, keep-it-to-yourself*. And there was no one else to look after me, those summers my parents were gone. Until we moved away entire, Nanni was the only one. My mother had a specialisation for Romance languages and literature and so she needed Europe – 'It's part of me', is what she always said. And my father, who was an historian, could always come follow her into some medieval town or other and make do, he'd find something to amuse himself with there while she was researching her book on unaffiliated sonnets, caesuras in sentences no one had even thought about before.

It's no wonder, when I think about it, that I stayed a child so long. There was the quiet talking of my parents, their ordered, oblong rooms, a life of universities and of books, with dainty cups and saucers laid out on a tray – set against that other louder, crying time in a place that had my mother's past in it . . . Of course it keeps you young, newborn, kind of. With all around you people turning secrets into stories you might never get to tell. I had to wait for the summers to come so that I could learn anything at all, fit the pieces in and watch out for little details, learn from my grandmother in words I could overhear, about my family, my *whenau*, with language and with hearing names of this one or of that one, someone they called *Wharakau* or sometimes Dick. Who was he, anyhow? I tried to figure it. That man they both loved? What was his real name or where was he now? Not asking, though, like children never really do ask, the big questions, if they're not knowing how the grown ups will act, how they'll be, when the replies came through. But watching my Nanni's face instead, when she and Queenie were talking in those sad crying times. Trying to understand. Trying to see.

*

That's how I went on, from summer to summer, surrounded by yellow hills, the thwack-thwack of the distant
train, the bleating of the sheep. There were the little new
fronds growing right up to our front door, green as green.
And we were together, my Nanni and me, just sitting or
talking or playing, making food, all one kind of known
and familiar life – so no need anyway, I told myself, to
go asking about the other mixed-up questions. 'No need,
sweetie' is what Queenie had told me, too, when I tried
to ask her once about my mother, why my mother stayed
away from her own mother the way she did. And why my
Nanni lived so on her own, not really knowing anyone in
the village where her own house was or seeing anyone but
only Queenie when Quennie came in. Why she spoke the
way she did, acted the way she did, so different from my
mother, in that language of hers that only her dear Lady
understood, half one thing, half another, those words of
hers that somehow had a body to them that took you on
its lap, took you in.

Queenie would bring something, every week, when
she came in and the nights she stayed on we'd all have
it for some kind of a big tea. Sweetcorn or a pig's leg.
Pumpkins. Plums from the wild fruit trees that grew up
behind her old house behind the *marae*. There they had
an old mighty vegetable patch she kept talking about,
set behind a *manuka* hedge to shelter it, and fed from
all the old water from the wash house and the chickens
that ran around there. That was a real garden, Nanni said.

Real Maori *kai* there and none of your *pakeha* little taters and mealy fruits. We should all go there and see it for ourselves. Real gardens, food. With earth around it, rain come down. 'My dream is one day I'll take you,' she said to me, 'when you're a big girl, and show you. When you're grown up, okay. A visit of our own and Queenie and Pete, we'll all go there together.'

But the years passed, and not as many of them as I like to remember, and I never went, to that place that stayed so far away and was somewhere for stories. Instead Nanni gave Queenie other kinds of food for her to take back there, tins of milk and biscuits that came in sealed wrappers, jars of jam and pickle you bought in the shops. So who was to know that where Queenie came from even existed, if I couldn't go there, or Nanni, but it was only Queenie who might belong? Who was to believe there was such a home where pigs ran around and then were killed, and people dug a hole in the ground and cooked them there with *kumera* and other vegetables, running crackling with the pig fat under hot, hot stones? Who was to believe that once upon a time a white girl had ever gone out there at all, met a *Maori* boy, and had a baby, fallen, fallen in love?

Anyhow I had my Nanni's garden, with the broccoli and beets and different kinds of lettuce, sweet potatoes, corn . . . She put them into stews. And she had up behind the ferny bank thick rose-bushes and beds of daisies, tall masts of bamboo keeping the flowers away from the bush, the gully and the scree. She had all this – so why go on and on about that other place, like it might hold meanings?

Why talk on about it with Queenie whenever the two of them got together? Like it was a place she might enjoy better than where she lived? Like it was a place she might need?

When I found out for sure the answers, it wasn't just the crying days that told me. Or overhearing Queenie say once about me that it may as well be I had no family, all because of 'that mother of hers' and Nanni saying 'or my big heart' . . . No, not even. It was the day when there were different kinds of tears, something not just crying but more than that, like wailing, calling, both of them together, Queenie putting her head back, I saw her do it and she closed her eyes.

Because Queenie had got sick, and soon after she was to die – this I learned years after my parents had moved abroad and there was a summer I never saw my Nanni, and after that not any summer, not ever again. After Queenie had gone and Nanni wiped her face, she took me in and told me like a poem, like something my mother might have said, constructed in a certain kind of way that it might be remembered and I have remembered it, all the words: 'How your mother's like a tree,' she said. 'And she wants to make herself into a tall clipped shape and straight, straight, when she could be so beautiful if she could grow differently, see, let herself be more wild. Come out thick at the base with strong roots,' Nanni said, 'and wide . . .'

'She lost herself,' I'd heard Queenie tell Nanni, in the low lamplight, that same day of the sickness and the wailing and the different kinds of tears; they'd been talking about my mother and my mother's father then. 'My brother would have loved her, man, if he'd stayed alive. But she's taken herself deep into the dry place, that daughter of yours. She doesn't know now', Queenie said, 'who she is.'

'And now I'm losing you, my Lovely Lady,' my Nanni said to Queenie in reply. 'You're leaving me. My last one left. All the *tangis,* they get started now.'

They hadn't known that I was there, that I had seen. I crept to the door and saw it all, heard it all, what they were saying. Saw Queenie take my Nanni in her arms. 'Honey, honey,' she said and she stroked her hair. 'You speak of this with me when you come out to the *marae,* eh? To say goodbye. When the little one's gone back to the city. I take you out there and remind you, honey, where you belong, where you and my brother always belonged . . .'

And they both were crying again then, for old days, old times, long ago and something sweet in it, something loved and lost, forever gone, crying, remembering, and wanting that time back, the person who gave you that time, grieving but having someone there to hold you in your grief, take you to their arms, go *Aueee* in a soft voice, keep you comforted so the spirits of your ancestors can come and give their comfort to you, take the sadness away.

The word for it is *tangi*, like Nanni said before, for sadness and for mourning, grief and loss. The summer I saw Queenie for the last time was when I found out why my Nanni loved her so. When I saw those tears, heard the kind of crying, saw the women sitting there . . . Sitting *tangi* for all they'd lost and were to lose, and remembering, remembering . . . Queenie the last part of her husband my dear Nanni had left.

And still there was my mother, sitting straight and unmoving in the front seat of the car, at the end of that summer, driving me away . . . What was she thinking, that she could remain that way, just so? Just sitting, just looking straight ahead at the road, her hands in position on the wheel? I wouldn't be writing any of this down now, I guess, if ever I knew what was going on in that one's head. And neither would it be a story then, would it? If I had it all in my mind from the beginning? I'd have nothing to find out, then, would I? In the writing? Have no need to tell?

For I am pale, my mother the dark one. Newborn, see? Like I might always stay too young to fully know. Newborn on account of those fronds, tiny curled-up toes and fingers, their new green. Newborn, like I was once and my mother and her mother before her, all of us, arrived curled up that way and closed into ourselves with the secrets of our birth like so many ferns kept huddled close together on that bank leading up to my grandmother's wooden house.

I guess in the end what made me understand the two places in my life was learning how I might live between them, that it might be okay to go from city to the country and back again, from the dark to light and the light to dark. From sentences all long with vowels and commas to other ways of being, other words . . . It might all of it be easy and okay.

Because now I know it's not so much as finding out the secrets, girl, as understanding where the words come from that makes a person who they are. And when I think about Queenie and my Nanni together . . . Well, something of that understanding started to make sense to me then, I guess. Something old, old, coming out of those two women's mouths and bellies and nothing in like it newborn. The way they spoke together on the step, the way they squeezed each other, or poked their fingers into each other's bellies and laughed . . . It was like watching whole bodies speaking, the old white woman and her *Maori* friend. Like all the understanding you might need coming deep, deep out of their real selves like the ferns right up at the back of the bank give up their seeds for new growth and everyone knew they'd been there a hundred years.

So, yeah.

Because a long time ago, sure, all this might have been another world.

But the story told by now, I guess, and listen to me now, you. How I sound.

Not so new, eh? After all?

*

Memorial

Not that she would ever put it this way, let alone turn it into something that might read like a story, but the fact is, when she starts thinking around the two events that seemed to mark the beginning and the end of her marriage, what she sees is one statue at one side and another at the other. Like bookends, is what the image is. And her life with Karl, those thirteen years in between when she was with him, they're like titles of books facing out of the shelf but she hadn't read any of them. All that time she'd never even looked inside.

And the statues were identical. Is how she remembers it, anyway. The same dead poet up on his box in the middle of a hot winter's day surrounded by foreign birdsong and strange trees as the one on the grey hill in the Borders that last weekend, after Karl had told her about his affair and how long it had been going on. He was still seeing her, he'd said, the woman he was involved with, but couldn't they make a go of things anyway? Because they were best friends, after all, him and her, they'd been like that since they met. And they liked doing the same things, didn't they, and wasn't that the most important part of marriage? To have interests in common? Isn't that what, Karl had said, kept people together in the end?

Like walking. That was how they'd met, at the University Rambling Club, and so quickly fell into the routine of going out to the hills in the weekends, coming back late or sometimes taking a tent with them in the summer months and staying out overnight. There was that exhaustion of lying down in their sleeping bags at the end of a long day and she can see now how that could have easily felt like deep contentment, happiness even. No wonder then he'd quickly called it love, Karl had, and she'd believed him. She'd ended up believing it for a long time.

Even that day when they were out in the Borders, after he'd told her about the woman he'd met who worked at the library and about all the time they'd had together and that he couldn't keep it secret any longer because he wasn't that kind of man . . . Elisabeth had not exactly realised at the minute of his confession that she would leave him as a result of it. For there it was still between them, the pleasure of the landscape, the miles they'd already come. She'd looked around her, from her place on the hill, taking in the lovely silence and the quality of the air, and yes the words Karl had said were there, but so too was the knowledge of the thermos in his rucksack, the delicious sandwiches she'd made that morning in hers . . . And nothing else had seemed as real as that, had it? The routine of their life together, it's childless, contented pleasures? She'd even said to him, hadn't she, as they'd stopped on the side of that hill and she'd looked all around her at the great bare expanse of wintry brown and grey . . . 'I think I understand what you mean . . .'

But then they'd walked on, and that's when she'd seen that the mark on the landscape which she'd noticed when they stopped and had thought was some kind of cairn or obelisk, was actually the statue of Robert Burns, and the same one – the other a copy of this perhaps – as the statue she'd seen all those years ago, on that holiday when Karl had asked her to marry him.

That holiday. You could say it had been like another part of their friendship too. It was the summer after they'd both graduated and they'd booked plane tickets straight away, making lists of what they'd need to take, walks they'd plan, with Karl organising every little detail. He'd made sure he could find the cheapest deal for one of those long-haul flights where you stop off everywhere in the world – the US and India. The Far East and Australia all the way to New Zealand and then home. He'd said it would be their big adventure, 'OE' they called it 'down under', meaning 'Overseas Experience' – like all the kids from New Zealand and Australia came through to Scotland for a year. Only this would be them having the adventure, leaving one side of the world for another, with nothing but their backpacks and their walking gear, all the money they'd saved, and, somewhere tucked into the corner of one of Karl's pockets, a tiny diamond ring.

Karl had told her, when they'd got home again, that
he'd always planned for it to be in New Zealand when
he would ask her to marry him, as far away as they could
be so that, as he put it, 'There'd be no going back.' Only
look at him, Elisabeth had thought that day in the Borders as they'd got closer to the statue and she realised it
was the same one: He had gone back on his word after all.
He'd gone right back. Though perhaps, she thinks now,
in another way, he'd only gone back to being the same
twenty-two-year-old he'd been when he'd said it was her
he wanted to be with all the time, sleeping with a young
woman every night and waking holding her tightly in his
arms like he was afraid she'd disengage herself from him
in the dark, that she'd quietly ease out one shoulder and
arm from the circle of his embrace and get away before he
saw her go out the door . . . Only that young woman was
no longer Elisabeth. It was someone else.

And that was when, when she'd come upon that statue,
something stirred in her then. But not because of him.
Not the sight of the dead poet up there on his plinth or
whatever it was called, with the dates of his birth and his
death and some half-worn-out bits of his poems beneath
his iron feet . . . It was something else, the memory of
another day with another statue, long ago, and of a sensation that she'd had then in the pit of her belly, ever since
Karl had given her the ring, like a little nub of hardness.
Like she'd swallowed the ring, been made to swallow it.
That Karl had not just put it in on her finger like he'd
done on some beach somewhere in the North Island but

had tilted back her head and poked it right down her throat like she was an animal and it was a pill . . . That's what she'd been thinking about the morning of the other statue. How being married felt like something she'd had to swallow. Though he'd asked her in a perfectly ordinary way and she'd said yes and now here they were in a different part of the country anyway and having had a row about directions because she'd been driving the hire car while he'd slept with the map on his knee and she hadn't woken him to ask him which way when the road had taken a fork around the base of that big mountain, what was it called, where they were supposed to be joining a walk that was setting off the following week . . . It sat with her as she'd driven, Karl quietly snoring beside her, continued to sit with her, the feeling of the little nub of Karl's will, sitting there in the pit of her and not dissolving.

He'd been cross when he woke because he liked to be in charge of that sort of thing, reading the map, giving instructions. Yet all the time while he'd been asleep she had loved it, just driving along the road and deciding which way to go as the signposts came up and choosing one way or another on the spur of the moment. She'd seen a sign that had in brackets under it ('Secret Lake') written up like that, like the title of a poem or a story, with speech marks around it as though it were someone's private, special name for a place, and it had a little picture beside it, a silhouette of a little figure and there in smaller writing underneath were the words 'Memorial to Robert Burns: ¾ mile' and an arrow. And she'd followed that.

They'd studied him in school of course, and Karl would have known a few of the poems by heart, no doubt, would have liked them too. But he hadn't been keen on the walk from the beginning. Waking like that to suddenly find himself somewhere that hadn't been planned for, wasn't in their itinerary, and yet there they were drawing up beside a picnic table and big municipal rubbish bin in a little car park dug out of the side of the road, with a board set up that gave walking directions to the lake and times it would take and the drawing of Burns and information all about him, and why he was Scotland's 'Most Loved Poet'.

Karl had stayed bad tempered while they pulled on their boots and jackets – jackets even though the winters were so mild there it was like summer at home, and people kept talking about the cold and sudden changes of weather but all Elisabeth could see was bright pacific blue sky all around her and the kind of sun that would make you brown if you lay in it and put suncream on. Not a winter at all. Even so, she did what he said, put her jacket on and they got ready in their usual way – and three quarters of a mile was nothing, she'd joked to Karl to cheer him up, they'd be in and out before he would notice they'd been gone.

They locked the car and headed into the opening in the bush that marked the beginning of a track. The bright day closed instantly behind them like a door. They were used to it by then, of course, from all their walks, the darkness, the close growth of the vegetation in this country that blocked out all the light. It had its own smell, its own particular damp and musky odour. You needed the tracks to be well marked or you'd be lost in a second, the low ferns and trees pushing in at you as you went deeper in and the high *totaras,* they were called, those amazing old and massive trees that grew not like trees growing in the woods at home exactly, but seeming to rise up out of all that other bush that was banked up around them . . . They made Elisabeth think of that line from another poet, nothing like Burns – 'Darkness visible.' Because that was what it was like there, looking into the dark, seeing the dark as your eyes adjusted, but as they walked on she didn't mind it either, Karl's back up ahead of her as the path inclined a little as though rising to a hill then flattening again. Certainly it had been an easy enough walk. The description on the board in the car park had not exaggerated the time it would take and after about twenty minutes she'd seen slices of bright water through clearings in the bush, the glinting reflections of the sun and then they'd stopped, Karl had, and she came up behind and he'd said, 'There it is', and there it was: 'The Secret Lake'.

Later, years later, once Elisabeth had started reading again and knew where 'darkness visible' came, in Book Two of *Paradise Lost* and why she'd always loved Milton, she'd found an essay by Rebecca West where she wrote about this lake. That had been like a secret, too, discovering that someone else knew about that place and had written about it. And she recognised the feeling that was described in the writing, of the surprise of seeing those sudden flashes of bright blue amongst the dark bush and then stopping and suddenly there it all was, this large and flat expanse of lakewater lying in the centre of the country, at its secret heart, wrapped around by *ponga* and *totara* and *manuka* all those trees and bushes she'd memorised the names of while she'd been there . . . A clear wide open lake of blue in a place that anywhere else in the world would have picnickers gathering on its little beaches, boats pushed off on the water's surface or water-skiers criss-crossing one side to the other – but here was completely hidden from view.

They saw the Memorial statue immediately – down one end of the lake and set like a jewel on a green lawn that had been created for it especially. They walked up towards it, skirting the water when the path took them down to the sand and then turning back into the bush for the final corner where they came out to stand on the grass. It seemed both bigger and smaller when they got there – the poet standing legs apart, hands on hips and his head upturned as though to catch the sun, high enough that you couldn't make out an expression on the face but low enough that the whole thing was of a scale that felt lifelike and real . . . Weirdly present, somehow, the figure of the famous Scottish poet set down here in this faraway country, polished and shining, with his own green lawn about him, even with the dark growth ever closer at his back, and the hidden lost water coming lapping over the sand towards the base of his pedestal where the dates of his birth and his death were marked, and those words again, after a few lines of his verse, 'Scotland's Most Loved Poet'.

Immediately she'd wanted to take off her jacket and stay. It was warm, now they were out here in this clearing, in the sun, the statue threw a clean dark shadow on the bright grass and Elisabeth had lain down alongside it, stripping off her top and trousers, the feel of the bright sun on her head and face and body like a pulse, a beat, the centre of the day above her and before her only blue . . . It did feel like summer, no matter what anyone in that country said, no matter what Karl said as he'd stayed standing there above her, alongside Robert Burns, refusing to lie down, to sit even. So she'd just stretched out, relaxed completely, the shadow of the poet beside her like a companion, her body long and lean and full of sun lying there on the grass.

She'd wanted to stay for the whole afternoon. She'd wanted to lie in the warmth and hear the lap, lap, lap of the blue water against the little beach, listen to the silence all around and the little sounds of birds she'd never heard before collecting in the tall trees. She'd wanted to stay all through the rest of the morning, into the afternoon, all through the day, let the sun come down and still she would stay . . . Not think about the next place they had to go to, or the next map to see . . . Not answer questions or make decisions, just keep herself whole in this state of absolute arrival she felt herself to be in now, like she'd felt in the car before with Karl asleep and she'd taken any turn she wanted, seen the sign and just followed it with her eyes. So it was like Karl may as well be asleep now. Like he wasn't even there. And she realised the little hard feeling in her stomach from before, that little bit of indigestible nut, like metal or bone, was gone and everything felt light and easy and warm.

That experience, she knows now, looking back on all this, of getting 'lost' on that holiday as Karl had said they were when he'd woken up to find himself somewhere unexpected, was of not being lost at all. It was the feeling, at the minute of letting it fall over her and claim her as she lay on the grass, of herself, of who she was, what she wanted, what she didn't want. That she didn't want to be pulled to her feet as Karl pulled her. Didn't want to go back into the bush and leave it all behind her, the bright open secret of the lake with its strange statue that had been like some kind of a marker, to make her feel that all was tended, the grass cut around it and the ironwork polished and cleaned so it glinted in the sun . . .

Still she had let herself be taken, her jacket draped back around her bare form, her trousers put into her arms. She'd looked at the brand new ring on her finger and she'd started getting dressed, Karl calling ahead of her, 'Come on! Come on! This whole crazy thing has been a complete waste of time!'

But the recognition of what that day had meant did come at last, and in full, thirteen years later with the second statue and on a wintry hill in Scotland, the only 'proper place', Karl had said, on that last walk they ever took together, 'for a statue of Robert Burns to be'. And there he was, she thinks now, and she's pretty sure it was the same statue, remember? Is how this all began. Only the second statue was not cared for and polished like the other in that other secret place, but had lichen smattering its tired body and on the base of the stand the words not clear nor the numbers for the dates as they'd been worn away by weather, all those details gone. A sort of fence had been put up around it, why? To stop people getting too close? To stop them harming the statue in some way? Who knows, but whatever the reason there was to be no lying down here in its shadow. No peace of silence, of bush and then the water and then the green.

And that's when she said to Karl, like she should have said to him that day long ago by the water, 'No.' He was still talking. Talking as he stood. As though she'd never spoken. Talking like he'd talked all the way on the walk across the cold hills, still making his confession, but saying over and over they would make a 'go of it anyhow' – wouldn't they? Old friends that they were, such great old friends. That they had that to remember, no matter what. All the interests they had, the hobbies they shared. It's what they had to hold on to, to go on with, what they had to keep . . .

But then she said it again, like she should have said it before, no. Finally saying it so he would hear. No. No point in remembering. No point in going on. And no, as well, to hold on to. And no, as well, to keep. No. No. And No. No, no, no, no and again no. Like the books in the bookshelf between the two bookends that stood like little statues either side might all have pages inside them all filled with the single word. No. She'd twirled her ring, dropped it on the grass. And Karl was down on his hands and knees to hunt for the speck of stone in the heather while she was walking away.

*

Dick

I was still fresh from my parents' divorce when my father gave me a car and taught me to drive. It was just before school broke up for the summer and getting hot, and I was too young to be out on the road on my own but my father knew all kinds of people in our small town and he had, as he put it, 'conversations'. Like he had them with his ladies and his friends, certain conversations about money deals and business debts, so my father could get what he wanted in his life, so he could get his way.

Until that time of the car, though, these kinds of things hadn't occurred to me. I was somewhat held back, you might say, was the reason – made younger than my years by my father and the way he carried on. That's what my brother Michael said. We were both pretty wrecked, Michael said, he and I, by our old dad and our mother leaving home and moving abroad and it turned out we wouldn't see her again for another fifteen years. So I may be living in the world now like everyone else with my own profession and my little tidy flat, but part of me is still that same girl from back then, learning to use the clutch then go first gear, second. Slowly driving on my own down the street where we lived.

There was a boy next door who I used to watch from my bedroom window and dream that one day he might look up as I came carefully past him, practising in that too-fancy brand new convertible of mine. He had a car of his own, an old lovely car, and would be out the front of his house working on it, an older boy with long blond hair that straggled down his back and the way he stood there in the sun in those beaten-up old jeans he wore and T-shirts that hung just anyhow . . . Even now the feelings I have about him mean I could never say his name.

My father didn't know anything about this. He just had the driving instructor pick me up after school each day and start the lesson there – as I turned the ignition and put the car in gear. Then we drove back to the house and my father paid him and made me go up and down the streets myself, around the block and over the hill by the shops. Certain times he even came with me, my father, that's how much he wanted me to drive. He'd be sitting right beside me in the tiny seat of the fancy car he'd bought for me as a gift, telling me this way or that, giving instructions on what to do at a set of lights . . . But always looking at his watch, too, and wanting to get back – 'to some little chickie he had waiting upstairs' were my brother's words. Or something else he needed to do. Still, those few times with him were times I felt close, when he said 'clutch now' or 'reverse'. And even on the days he didn't come, I thought I could sense his affection in the way he would wave me off goodbye. As if he was pleased to think that soon I'd be in that car for ever and I'd be driving away.

So the two weeks passed before school broke up and twice I went out and the boy in the street was waiting, kind of – is how I wanted to believe it was. Hanging around by his car as I drove past him in my own. And twice I saw him look up as I passed, push the yellow hair back clean from his face as I went from second gear into first while time seemed to slow down and then stop, with the blue of that tall boy's eyes upon me. Me thinking, in that moment, how it might be to get someone to love you. To let your mouth go wide open so another person could come in.

But I didn't see the boy in the street after that – or if I did, I don't remember. Because something went wrong with the car – something, my father said, that was to do with the engine and that it would need to go into the garage straight away. 'There are often problems', he said, 'with these little convertibles. You can get a bit of trouble with the brakes and stopping suddenly.' I remember exactly how he looked at me then, my old handsome dad. He was on his way, I remember, out the kitchen door. 'I'll take it into the garage today,' he said, 'and you can pick it up later, after school. Dick's a friend of mine. He does the work himself on all my cars. He'll do yours in a day and you can drive it home after on your own.'

*

That was a long time ago, a morning when everything changed for me like it had changed for my brother before me but he never talked about it, he just never left his room, stayed in there with the light on in the dark. A lifetime, you might say, and a day with all of my life locked inside it, a secret I would never tell. Even my mother, when I finally saw her, was not someone I could reveal myself to, to show myself that way. When we met each other, after all that time of her being gone, we were both of us strangers. But I do remember how she said, 'You don't surround yourself with certain kinds of people and not feel the consequences.' Is what my mother said. 'Except your father, well . . . He just found a way of not letting himself know the effects of anything he did. Or what those so called "friends" of his might do.'

She was right, of course. For the last time I drove was that day coming back from Dick's garage, and my father as long as he lived never did ask me why. Though he was the one who'd fixed it, that it would turn out for me that way. He'd given me the car after all, when I was too young, arranged that it would need to go into the garage that day, and that the garage would be empty, with no cars at all, no men, no customers around when I walked into the empty yard. There was the sign 'Richard Clarke and Co.' over the entrance but only one man there in the dark office waiting. *Dick's a friend of mine.* 'And I've been waiting for you,' he said.

And so I'm left here with the memory of it, fitting in the pieces, all grown up now and old, and my poor brother still in that place where they keep him like he's a child. And my father long dead and the girlfriends gone and my mother, after she spoke with me that day, never did come back . . . And you try to understand, don't you? They say: Write down your stories and you'll come to a kind of learning. Write all the way to the end. Read the story out loud.

But what I'm left with now is no different to what I had when I began: A set of keys, a 'conversation'. A gift. Some kind of start but really with no words to follow. And so you know why there's something wrong with me by now, why the boy in the road is a dream, why my brother stays inside. Why I don't go up to people, don't get close. Something that comes from that mess all over my clothing that day, of oil and other stuff, and my father walking down the hall towards me when I got home . . . After all that happened, all that he let happen . . . Calling out to me and smiling . . . With some fresh lovely shirt on, and he says, 'Hi honey? Everything gone okay?'

That comes from knowing then what he knew – that he'd given me too, I was one of his 'gifts', my old powerful handsome dad – but was never, ever going to say. What price had been fixed. What debt I'd paid. What Dick had done.

*

Infidelity

The morning, when she stepped out into it, felt new minted, as though everything the day would need had been printed fresh. The grass was that bright green you get in the very early morning sunshine, and the leaves on the trees, each one seeming particular and exact, glistened like pieces of tin, the sky the kind of blue that looks as though someone had taken a cloth to it and polished it, rim to rim.

'New minted' – that was the phrase that came to her, precisely, the minute she stepped outside. The little house was dark at her back, Richard inside sleeping. But here on the front porch the whole day presented itself to her and all at once, the river beyond the gate a delicious slip of silver in the brightness of the early light.

Her thought had been – what? To go swimming, just that. To get straight into that delicious water that she'd known was flowing along there, right outside the front of the house. Yes, that is what she'd intended. She's writing all this down now, years and years after, the children are at school and she gives herself this time, three mornings a week, to work on her fiction. The class she goes to is all about that: Regular writing time, setting aside a particular day, a particular place, and returning, over and over, to that established routine. Her professor, a woman in her mid-sixties with a rope of long grey hair running down her back in a thick plait, is possibly the most inspiring person Helen has ever met. 'Regular writing time!' – that's her mantra. 'You'll get nothing finished, you'll be nothing but talk, if you don't find the time, regularly, through the week, to start and work through a project.'

So – 'Here we go!' Helen says to herself now, thinking about that, getting the title down, 'Infidelity', and that first line about the morning. She knows exactly what the story will be about. It's not a story at all, actually, but something that happened to her seventeen years ago, the first day of her honeymoon, right after she and Richard got married. She might have to change the names in the story later, she's thought about it in advance, switch around a couple of things. And there are scenes she can surely add that will turn the whole thing into fiction, in the end. She can do that. She will certainly do that.

For now though, let the lovely morning run. How beautiful it had been. Late June and the weather is always beautiful in the Highlands then. She'd got up very, very early and slipped on a dress, not bothering about underwear or shoes. Really? Yes, really, 'not bothering', though it seems extraordinary that she could go out that way when she was always so careful about everything, so thorough. But then, it really was the most extraordinary day. There had been rain in the night, she'd heard it after Richard had gone to sleep. They'd been up, late as late, fooling around. Having a laugh actually. Sex on your honeymoon, after all – the whole thing was so corny and sweet. As had been the wedding before it, the huge, huge wedding, that big wonderful fuss. Finally it had been over and they'd managed to get away, driven up here, got in around midnight.

'I can't see anything,' she'd said to Richard when they'd arrived. The countryside was so dark where they were, a remote part of Scotland way off on the west coast. The roads were impossible, they wound and narrowed. Up hills, down hills. Looming mountains off there somewhere in the distance, and somewhere else nearby the sea. There wasn't a single village, a street with street lights; there wasn't a single light for miles around.

'I can't see!' she'd said again, when they went inside the little house they'd rented for two weeks.

'You're not supposed to see,' Richard had replied. 'It's your honeymoon, remember? The whole thing is supposed to be a surprise.'

And it was. In the exact way honeymoons are supposed to be a surprise. Because when she'd stepped outside for the first time that morning, there it had been, set out for her like a picture, just as Richard had said it would be – the dear little riverside lodge they'd come to, with its porch and steps going down to a big square garden at the front, planted with borders of daisies and pinks and there, too, just beyond the gate, the river. The Elgin. One of the most beautiful rivers in the world, Richard had told her, and he knew. He knew about rivers.

'It's true, I might *show* the water a fly or two,' he'd said when they'd been discussing it, before the wedding. 'It would be crazy to have a week at a place like that and not take the fishing with it.'

'I should think so,' Helen had replied. She quite liked fishing herself. It was one of those things she and Richard talked about doing as they grew old together, somewhere in the future when they would have lots of time on their hands. Her father had made a speech about it at the wedding, about all the months and years they would have with each other now that they were married, and he'd finished with a toast that ended with the words, 'Tight Lines!'

So, of course it would make sense to fish here as well as picnic and walk and swim. They were going to have a wonderful time. She loved the west coast, and Richard knew this little place. He and his family had come here once when he was a boy.

'I've found us somewhere really lovely, darling,' he'd said.

Exactly that, those words: 'I've found us somewhere really lovely, darling.' She wants to get these details in, to the story she's writing. The class is next week so she wants to have as much down on paper now as she can.

'Essential details,' Louisa had said, in the last session. 'Don't worry too much about what will happen. Let your essential details pull you along, let them accrue. In time, they'll make the story for you. It will be natural, an organic process.' She'd given them masses of Grace Paley and Carson McCullers and Virginia Woolf – the very, very short stories – to read as inspiration. And Tennessee Williams, who, as she'd said earlier, writing the letters out in capitals in the air, she happened to 'ADORE'. For his raggedy little sentences, she said. 'For the little itty bitty ways, his bits and pieces add up. For letting idiosyncrasy win the day.' She'd shaken her long plait then and laughed. She'd let Sam Shepard's stuff in for the same reason, she said, the plays as well as the short stories. 'He's someone else who knows how to let what people do create the narrative, not some author or other.'

But what if, Helen thinks now, that author is also the person in the story, who knows in advance what's to come? Like she knows now what's to come in this short story? When she knows because all of this happened to her, because she's writing from life?

'Just follow the details,' she hears Louisa say. 'Try not to think about what's going to happen before it's happened.' Concentrate on the here and now, then get back to the beginning and follow through. What were you doing that first morning of your honeymoon that you want to write about it now? Can you tell me about that, please?

'Yes,' says Helen out loud. She has pages of white paper in front of her, all stacked together neatly on her desk. The house is in order, and everything has been arranged, she's made space in the daily planner, cleared the diary, so that she can spend the time doing this, working on her writing. It can't have been more than six in the morning, earlier maybe. The birds were clattering away in the garden, the sound of them was amazing. They talk about a dawn chorus – well, this was it, all right. Helen stopped, her bare feet on the wet grass, and looked up at the trees. The leaves were rustling with activity and birdsong, fluttering feathers. A blackbird shot into a tall Scots pine and disappeared amongst the foliage. There was another eruption of song. It was quite simply one of those kinds of days that had been made to be perfect. The birds knew that. The trees did. It was as though the whole world had been waiting for the moment the new bride would step out of her house and partake of its wonders. Helen is pleased with that thought; it's to be a central theme of the story. She put her face up to the sun, and felt its warmth already, this early. She was the new bride. The whole day was going to be extraordinary. She would go for a swim and then it could start.

She didn't have a watch on that morning, she must have taken it off for the wedding and kept it off, which was a bit irresponsible, but yes, it would have been six or earlier. It had been raining in the night and that's why the light was so clear and shining. It's why the birds were so alive, the river such a clean slip. Everything was rinsed and polished and awaiting her. A new world for a new bride, like a fairytale, like a myth. Helen laughed at the conceit of the whole idea. To be a new bride – that on its own, in this day and age! And the big wedding the day before, the speeches. Her father acting as though she was a little girl, her mother crying even, in the church – she'd seen her!

'For goodness' sake, Mum!' Helen had said afterwards, when they were getting ready for the photographs. 'It's not such a big deal, is it?'

'I know, my love,' her mother had replied, and she'd smoothed back a strand of Helen's hair and tucked it into the veil, her eyes searching her daughter's face and then welling up with tears again. 'I know,' she'd said. 'I can't help it.'

But that's because the whole thing *had* been a big deal. It had been a huge wedding. It had cost a fortune. The entire ceremony start-to-finish like an ad for a wedding, actually, with everything just as she'd wanted it to be, with the flowers and the candles and the bells ringing – yet who would have known the performance of it could turn them into such players! And she and Richard acting out their part. Her wedding dress, after all. Her 'Going Away Outfit'! It was exactly like the movies, the magazines – when she and Richard had been living together beforehand, for goodness' sake. They'd known each other for nearly five years. They'd planned everything; everyone had always known they were going to get married. So it shouldn't be such a big deal, should it? Well it shouldn't have been but it was. Which is why Richard had wanted the honeymoon to be really low key. 'Somewhere we can just drive to afterwards,' he'd said, when they'd been talking about it. 'Somewhere mellow, super easy. So that we can leave the wedding and just go, no overnight hotels, flights, nothing. Don't worry, I'll figure it out.'

Richard, Richard, Richard. Maybe she should call the story 'Richard', not 'Infidelity' at all. Because he is like the anchor here, Richard is, the one that made everything that happened believable, real. Just imagine if Helen was writing about some other couple, some other woman . . . None of it would feel as though it had actually happened, would it, not quite authentic or true? She might not even be able to write it down. But with Richard here, in the middle of things, her own husband – well, it was like making sure the facts were straight, having something ordinary and commonplace to begin with, the history of their lives together at her back, the way they'd always wanted the same things, had the same ideas about life, their wedding, the honeymoon. And he'd encouraged her to take the writing course in the first place, Richard had, now that the children were older, and she didn't need to be at home all the time, looking after the house, looking after them. She could take a class or two, get a job later doing some kind of writing if she wanted. She'd always wanted to write, hadn't she? Well then, here was her chance, starting with this story – the first that she is completing, start to finish, for the class next week. Everything else before has been only an exercise, a preparation for this. Louisa hasn't allowed them to so much as imagine writing a whole short story until now, halfway through the first term. 'Just follow the details,' is what she said at the end of that last session. 'Get back to the beginning and follow through.'

Inside, Richard was still asleep. Much earlier, in the bedroom, in the dark, Helen had lain beside him, listening to the sound of his breathing.

'My husband,' she had thought, and it felt so nice, so comforting and real, to have those words echoing in her mind that she had whispered them out loud, like a secret, felt the shape of the syllables in her mouth, the press of the consonants against her lips. 'My husband.' And then, later, she'd heard the sound of rain, and then must have slept for a while. Because the next thing she knew, her eyes were open and there was light coming in through a slit between the curtains, through the partly opened window she could hear birdsong, and she was up and dressed, but no shoes on, no underwear.

'Detail, all detail,' says Helen. Because that detail *is* important, isn't it? Like the fact that she was barely dressed because she intended to go for a swim, that she'd prepared herself for it, to be exposed, somehow, open to the day. That she would take herself out that way, go out at a strange hour and find a part of the river that was deep and dive in. Go into the water and then come back and get into bed with Richard, naked and damp and cold, and Richard would wake up then, he would turn to her, in his way, say sleepily, 'Oh, hello you . . .' Yes it was what she'd wanted. To leave him sleeping in the dark house, and then return.

Richard. Richard was lovely. The wedding had been lovely. This place he'd found for them was lovely, too, exactly as he'd said it would be. They'd seen nothing of it last night because he'd kept the lights off as part of the surprise and they'd had to feel their way to the bedroom, to the bed. The curtains were drawn, but the housekeeper had left the window slightly ajar so the air could come into the room and allow the night-time in, its small noises, intimate and soft . . . And in the morning, when she'd woken, Helen could see how lovely it all was, all of it properly organised, the way the housekeeper, her name was Isobel, had arranged things for them, with milk and bread and coffee in the refrigerator, sweet peas in a jug on the kitchen table. And outside, there was the beautiful garden with its borders thick with daisies, and lilies and roses, all kinds of plants growing you didn't normally see in gardens in the Highlands.

But it was sheltered, wasn't it? Where they were? The sea half a mile away and a high hedge to the side to protect it from northerly winds . . . No wonder you could plant anything here. The whole place was so cut off from the rest of the world, unlike anywhere else, it was all so special. Helen opened the little gate and there, directly in front of her, was the river. 'It was like having a river outside your front door,' she used to say to the children, how many times, when they were small, wanting to hear the story of her and Richard getting married. 'It was a dear little house with a garden and a gate and beyond the gate was the river,' she would say. Often finishing with, 'I'll take you there, some day', but knowing, absolutely, that she never would. For there it was, the Elgin, flowing by in easy slides of slow moving water, dark and peaty and inky blue, the bank on either side sloping down gently to form a little beach in one place, broken up with boulders and stones and meadowgrass in others, and central to this story of Helen's, and very, very beautiful, but also devastating, is the best word she can think of, to describe it, though she's not sure she will use that word in the story. In fact, she's not even sure why that word has occurred to her now. It's a terrible word.

'Your daddy was so clever to find such a magical place for our honeymoon,' she used to say to the children, all those years ago when they were small. Ella would have still been on her knee, the older two already started at school. How many more times would they want to hear about their parents' honeymoon? Ella took her thumb out of mouth to say, 'Honeymoon', then put it back in again. 'Yes, darling. Honeymoon.' Because of course it was a lovely thing to say, a lovely idea, honeymoon, and he was lovely, Richard was lovely. He thought of everything. He'd always been that way.

'I know exactly where we'll go,' he'd said, months before the wedding, over supper at home. 'For our honeymoon, Helen. I've got it all figured out. There's this place we went to when I was a boy. I can get the address from Mum and Dad, they'll still have it. Way off in the west, up north, and in a bit from the sea; it has its own river, well a stretch of it, the Elgin. And it's there right outside the gate. We can fish, we can swim . . . It's very private, no neighbours, no one around. We can just be on our own for the entire time. We don't need to see another single person. River Lodge, I think is what it's called, something like that. I'll find out.'

And he did, and he figured it all out, that they'd be able to drive there after the party, that he'd arrange with the housekeeper to have everything set up so they could just get there, late at night, and fall into bed.

'And two weeks to ourselves . . .' Richard had reached across the table for her hand, then gently drawn her around to his side of the table and she'd settled herself on his knee and they'd kissed.

'I'll be married by the time we get there,' Helen had said. 'It will be like this, the two of us together, but different.'

'I would have thought so,' Richard replied.

There was dew on the grass. Helen's bare feet had made beautiful prints across the lawn. New prints for a new day. A new bride. These were the kinds of thoughts, sentences, that were flitting through her mind. There, the footprints; the blackbird flying home to its tree. There, the brand new feeling of the day. 'New minted', remember? She'd been accounting for individual moments, descriptions, as she experienced them one by one that morning as she unlatched the gate of the garden, and stepped beyond it, on to a little gravelly path that gave way to grass. She remembers how, that morning, certain phrases – new bride, new minted, and so on – had actually occurred to her in words, one after the next, like words following each other on a page. And here she is now, years later, writing them down. Years and years. Four children later and the youngest now at secondary school so no more excuses that she has to be home all day, doing nothing but looking after the house, looking after all four of them and Richard, too. So she had taken the class she'd found out about online, with university accreditation, a proper writing course for people who knew about books, who were really interested in novels and short stories and had experience with their first degrees and so on, were mostly English Literature graduates. 'You've always wanted to have a shot at writing,' Richard had said, when they'd discussed it. 'Go ahead. Take the whole degree if you want to! Who knows what might come of it, darling?'

Richard. Richard, Richard, Richard. 'Oh, hello you,' he still said, sometimes, when she woke with him in the dark and they turned to each other, him cupping the ball of her shoulder with his hand like he'd always done.

'I love you very much,' she would say to him then.

'You two have such a great marriage, you've such a lovely home together,' Celia Walgrove told her, repeatedly, and Helen didn't even know Celia Walgrove that well, though she liked her enormously. They had met through school meetings and had got on from the start, she was Lizzie's best friend's mum – the girls would be going on to the same secondary school.

'You're so . . . connected,' Celia said. 'That's rare.' She herself had recently divorced. 'You and Richard. You're great together.'

As they were. Helen had known from when she'd first met Richard that they would always get on, like she knew she and Celia would get on, it was an instinct she had, a certainty about certain things, to arrange for the future in sensible ways, make plans that were realistic and that would add up and contribute meaningfully to domestic life. That morning in the Highlands, coming out on to the river, in the sun, she'd had the instinct for it then, of all that was to come. The contentment. The children. The long, long years. As though she and Richard had been able to be part of something that not everybody might gain access to or know about. She'd been aware of it even as she'd risen and dressed that morning all those years ago, known as she stepped out the door, to go into the water and be away from him and on her own . . .

'You two make me understand why people can stay married,' Celia would say. 'You make the whole thing work.'

It was going to be a lovely summer. As she left the little garden behind her, River Lodge and its flowerbeds and lawn, Helen could feel the months of sun and gardens and green grass stretched out in front of her. The trees were in heavy, heavy leaf. June weddings were the nicest, everybody said. In England or in Scotland, the weather was always the most reliable. Long evenings, masses of light. She and Richard had agreed ages ago, ages ago, that when they got married they'd get married in June. The house, the garden, everything this time of year was at its best, beautifully kept. She might have organised it that way herself, the kind of planting and the flowers that had been selected, the arrangement of the path and the little white gate. In fact, Helen thought, once upon a time this place might have been lived in by a couple just like her and Richard, imagine it, some other unknown new bride rising early on a summer's morning to make a sort of pact with her future – it might be another kind of story. How the other one, too, would have had shoulder length brown hair, would favour cotton dresses like she wore. She, too, would have wanted to have had four children, first a boy, just as it should be, then the three girls, be married to a man who was tall and skinny and wore glasses for driving. Who had a sweet habit of screwing up his nose when she was explaining something lengthy and complicated to him, about the children or schools or their arrangements for the week, going through their diaries and matching up all the dates in the calendar, acting like he wasn't sure he knew what she meant when she was using the special stickers that came with the daily planner, this particular one for this activity, this for another, so that he had to answer her very, very slowly.

'Okay, so if I've got this straight, you're telling me . . . ?'

It's all detail, Helen thinks now. The way Richard's nose crinkled, as she's just written. The fact that he's always worn glasses for driving. Her organised life with him and the children, though keep the stuff about the children to a minimum, they weren't part of this story. Except that Lizzie was big enough now to start secondary school which is why Helen can be writing in the first place and Ella two years ahead of her, and then Rose, and David about to finish school altogether . . . But no. This wasn't about family, it was about the first day of her marriage. 'Infidelity'. The title had come to her, like it might not just be a short story but a whole collection of stories. A cycle of stories, even, with a theme running through them about the kinds of secrets people have, the quiet, secretive things they do. So, 'Infidelity' it had always been. Not 'Richard'. 'Infidelity' from the start, with Helen waking alone on the first morning of her marriage and the river there, just outside the gate, like a long bone running through the centre of the story and giving shape to it and structure, and meaning something, yes, it was crucial to this narrative, to the way events played out, because as she started to walk upriver that morning, walking along the bank to find the perfect place to dive in and have her swim, Helen turned a bend and there ahead of her in the distance she saw someone, he was fishing.

Or he had been fishing, and had already put down his rod.

Or he wasn't fishing. He'd never been fishing.

It doesn't matter. The only thing that is significant here, that counts for anything as far as Helen's writing project is concerned, is that the minute he saw her he started coming towards her.

Infidelity

*

It occurs to Helen now that she might have opened the story at this point: With a man fishing on the riverbank, who was drawing in his line and at that moment saw a young woman walking in his direction. Or, that he saw her and then pulled in the cast, laid down the fly rod he'd been holding on the bank and started towards her. Because from the beginning, she could write, it was as if he knew her. The way he came to her with such purpose – at first in the distance, but within seconds getting closer and closer, near enough that she could see the kind of man he was, exactly, his build, his age, his character, and that for her, for Helen, in those moments as she watched him, though it shocked her, a stranger coming for her that way, she wasn't frightened at all.

'It was as though you'd been waiting for me,' she said to him, seconds later, when he was by her side.

'I know,' he replied.

But wait. Helen stops, puts down the pen. Not that.

'Go back to the beginning,' Louisa says, and that's what she's done. 'The morning, when she stepped out into it, felt new minted' – that was the sort of story it was supposed to be, and she's finished that section, it's done. As organised and sorted as her linen cupboard, she might say, and that was exactly as it should be, too. So don't start thinking now about another order of events, changing the content that way. Because she was always to start with something that was real, was supposed to be real – the memory of a strange morning by the beautiful river and a moment that she had entered into, fully, all those years ago. Like taking off her dress and going into cool water. That was to be the story's centre, always, its beginning and its heart. Then, the plan was, she would add to it, put something in that would turn the whole thing into fiction – a confrontation, a kiss. Call it 'Infidelity'. There would be an embrace, an affair, something dramatic and passionate . . . Something. She's taking classes in creative writing, for goodness' sake. Not 'It was as though you'd been waiting for me', as she's just written, not 'she wasn't frightened at all'.

Well, they're there now, those phrases, so just leave them for now, for the sake of moving the story along, and let it be enough to write that she saw him clearly, this unknown man, saw him for the first time when he reached the place where she was standing on the riverbank. Then she can describe: A tall man, well built, slightly overweight, slightly stooped. Dressed in fishing gear – though he carried none of that with him when he came. Helen had just been standing there, watching him get closer, and closer as he came towards her. She remembers there was the texture of the grass under her bare feet, some mud. She was, after all, right by the deepest part of the river, at a place where she might swim. The water, as she stood there, ran along beside her all in a piece, inviting her in, and seconds ago she would have taken off her clothes and walked into the slow, lovely current.

And 'embankment' . . .

What a word that is, a wonderful word. She might think more about that, 'embankment', and its position here, in the story. That would be a useful thing to do. More useful at this point than trying to work out whether this scene or that should feature, or when exactly she is planning to have her story veer off into the imagination. Think instead about that detail of her standing upon the embankment – as though the embankment might hold her in place for a while, stop her going forward. Helen realises she's starting to see the whole story more and more as a construction, actually, made up of her memory, of what happened that morning, and of the words she's using to describe it, of further words. So, the river. Embankment. This man who'd been further upstream, he might have been fishing. These are all important words. Yet the words are getting in the way of what she wants to tell, too, in the story, as though holding up the direction of it, where it should be going, and instead exposing something else within – as though exposing of herself – like wearing nothing beneath the cotton dress, and no shoes and already her feet were in slippers of mud, her long bony feet coated in it, as she stood on the embankment watching him come towards her. And, 'embankment', again. See? She wants to stop the story right here with that word. It is a beautiful, beautiful word. It rises up before Helen like a bed and all she wants to do is lie down. To put her arms around this man she's never seen before in her life, to breathe in his warmth and scent, put her arms around him and let him bring her down.

*

She stops writing. What is happening? For none of that is to be in the story. Only what is real, remember? What actually happened, and then add something, and an ending. That's what she's supposed to do. Start with the memory of what happened and go on from there: That he came towards her as though he recognised her, as though she were someone he thought he knew. Though he didn't know her. Though they were strangers to each other, strangers. Still, there she was. There he was. And he had been fishing, hadn't he? Hadn't she seen that first? A figure silhouetted slightly against the light – against the golden, printed glint of it. Helen knew enough about fishing to know that if he had been casting he must have already brought in his line, laid down his rod, to have come so quickly towards her after he'd seen her. Or if he hadn't been fishing he'd just been waiting for the moment she would come around the bend and then he would start heading towards her, straight away. Thinking about it, Helen decides, the story might be better if he had indeed been fishing. It makes his presence there on the riverbank more credible, doesn't it, at that hour of the morning? That makes it more real? She could write that it was because he was fishing that they were both so quiet, why they didn't call out, one to the other. 'Hi there!' or 'Are you our neighbour at River Lodge?' Something like that, noisy chatter, conversation. Because to be quiet beside the water, it was how one went about it. Fishing required quiet and stealth. She'd learned all that from Richard, from her father. She liked fishing, fly fishing from a bank. Off a little boat, sometimes. She liked all the talking about it, about flies and weather and the time of year. So yes, that could have been why he came to her. To let her know in advance there was a fish there, a big salmon lying in a pool, so would she please be very, very quiet or else go away. That's it, Helen thinks. Obviously he must have set aside his gear so that he could come down the embankment to tell her –

'No,' Helen says aloud, because 'details', remember? Louisa's rule? Every detail had to be there but every detail also had to be true. And what is true is that there was no fish, no excuse, no other reason than what's already written. He'd arrived, to be with her, that's all Helen needs.

'It was as though you'd been waiting for me,' she has written.

And—

'I'm sorry to come up on you like this—'

He might have said.

She's written that, that he said that.

But actually she has no memory of what he said, that moment when he got to her, what she might have said, because all she's aware of is that he'd come straight to her from where he'd been, came right up close to her, was so close, and she was going to put her arms about him, she was going to press her face against the side of his warm neck, breathe in the scent of him, feel the warmth of his skin. And so it may have been that he thought she was someone else, that he came down to meet her because he thought she was another woman, not her, and said to her then, 'Oh, I'm sorry. I'm hopeless without my glasses. I see I've made a mistake,' and so also it may have been that she has written that she said to him, 'It was as though you were waiting for me' – these things don't matter. Now that she's sitting here with the pen, the paper. She realises she has no concrete memory of anything to write down at this part of the story other than to record his scent, the golden colour of him, of his throat, of his arms. He was wearing a soft, dark green shirt, the sleeves pushed up to the elbows, and a vest, a fishing vest . . . But are these the kinds of details that matter, Louisa? Do they add up at all? Helen is doing the best she can, but this was not necessarily how the story was supposed to go. Only that he was a stranger, was the idea in the first place, and that this might be how something could start, between a man and a woman, that she could imagine, could make up . . . Which was why she could even think about writing any of this in the first place. Changing the names, probably, and a few other things. She could only think about writing a story called 'Infidelity' that Richard might read because the dramatic content of it would be invented, fiction. Because otherwise what happened to her that morning of the first day of her marriage doesn't make a story at all, does it?

Does it?

'What?'

She can write that down. That when he said, 'I'm sorry to have come up on you like this—' she replied, 'What?' She could write herself saying that to him, that word, and the way every second of their meeting was like every second articulating itself within the vast spread of time, and her imprisoned within each one.

'What?'

And details such as his tanned arms, the soft shirt. Is that the 'little itty bitty important stuff' that Tennessee Williams always made to be the centre of his work, the way Louisa says? Little monologues, scraps of dialogue enough like Sam Shepard has little scraps of dialogue, but then he writes big speeches too.

And that he said, 'I saw you from up there, from a distance.' She can write that.

And that she said to him, somewhere, amongst all the other sentences, but maybe have it appear much later, 'It was as though you'd been waiting for me.' Maybe that? Though she's not sure she should have herself ever saying that to him in the story. Or if she does, maybe later. Maybe put it in much, much later . . .

Or change the whole tone of the story altogether: What about doing that? That she'd been about to turn around and head back to the house when she saw him. Because anyone who's fishing from the bank loathes disturbance, we know that by now. And so Helen had been about to go back to the house, back the way she came, but then his voice had called out to her, 'Hi!' and he'd waved at her – so there, more details there, realistic details, more dialogue – he was simply calling out to her, he didn't mind about calling out at all.

It could have been like that, too.

'Hi!' he called out to me, in a friendly voice, Helen writes, but has to cross it out. The story is in the third person, remember? That has to be part of it. 'When I release you into fiction, I release you into the third person, past tense ONLY,' Louisa had said, writing ONLY in capitals in the air again. 'No stream of consciousness. No I-do-this and then-I-do-that . . . I want you to interrogate your details,' she'd said. 'I want you to be rigorous about them. I want your readers to read EVERY word along the line – like Lawrence says we must do – the sentence must LIVE along the line. None of that skimming, summative yeah-yeah-I-get-it kind of story. I want your readers following every one of your sentences, every detail, every single word.'

But what about repetition? Helen worries about that like she worries about the role of the author in a story. She's been worried about repetition from the very first class when they did a workshop exercise based on one sentence, and they had to rewrite it in five different ways, but when she brought it up, that repetition might be boring for the reader, Louisa had just put her hand towards her, palm outwards, and said, 'Virginia Woolf, Helen.' Helen is thrilled and inspired by most of the things Louisa says, the way she says them. That writing may as well be the same as living for someone like Louisa, that there may be nothing whatsoever dividing the two – this is an idea that's never occurred to Helen before she started taking this class. It would never have occurred. She decides then that she must understand from her teacher's remark that repetition is okay if the writer is aware of using it for reasons of rhythm and shape. And what's more, repetition, as Louisa has reminded her, can be part of writing as it is part of life. Still, there are some readers who are not like Louisa, who might get bored with it, mightn't they? Helen is aware of this dilemma, and continues to worry about it, about different kinds of readers and their expectations of a story – even though she also knows, and even without Louisa here to show her, that her own story cannot move on, can only . . . enlarge . . . is how she thinks of it, if she does go back and around, re-approach what happened that day long ago, come at it from different angles . . . And come at it again. Because it was surely an event, a narrative event, the meeting that took place between her and that unknown man all those years ago, but it's also lacking . . . 'authorial push' – another phrase from Louisa that seems relevant here. As in, 'For godsake, that wrecks a story completely, knowing some author is there in the background, fiddling and planning and scheming and pushing the whole thing along.' So maybe what Helen is doing here is all right, after all? Letting everything just hang?

She doesn't know anything. She's put down her pen.

All she knows is what she'd known then: Only, Yes. Yes and yes and yes. Anything.

*

'Stop! Don't go!' he'd called, had he? Had she made to turn? 'I'm coming to you, there', and she had waited for him, just as he said. She watched him getting closer and closer and when he arrived she could smell the warm, deep smell of him, the tang of his sweat from running, could see the softness of his shirt, the brown tan of his arms, and—

'Wait right where you are,' he'd said when he was just a few feet away and when he reached her, he put out his hand, not to shake her hand but to touch her wrist, encircle it with his fingers, like a bracelet or a cuff and she was utterly, utterly unafraid.

'It was as though you'd been waiting for me,' she might have said then. That might have been the moment. When she wanted to put her arms around him, put her face up against the side of his face, let him bring her down with him on to the soft bank.

Helen picks up her pen, lets him encircle her wrist again with his fingers. When he'd touched her, she'd felt the jolt of it.

'You're in the cottage,' he said. 'Up at River Lodge. You're staying there, aren't you? Isobel told me, I live there . . .' He gestured with a nod to somewhere in the distance, beyond some trees. 'Isobel is my housekeeper, too,' he said. 'She told me you were staying for a week or so, with your husband. I was going to come along to introduce myself, to say hello. But then, just now . . . You see, I thought you were someone else.'

Lightly, lightly he held her wrist and it was the most natural thing in the world.

'It's strange, isn't it?' Helen said to him.

'Exactly,' he said.

And he leaned in then, towards her, and she reached towards him . . . And, what? Was she going to kiss him then? Was he going to kiss her? What was going to happen now? That he leaned down towards her, and that she reached up, she put her face up to his face . . . And she'd thought, Yes. And yes and yes . . . Will she write that down? Even though they had never met each other before? That he'd only come for the way he did because he thought she was someone else? Even though they didn't know each other and were complete strangers, still there was this moment of him leaning down towards her and . . .

But instead she did not reach up.

She broke from him and ran away.

Though it's not what she'd intended.

For the story, she means. For the story. That she broke from him and ran, and ran and ran and she didn't look back, all the way home to the little house, and arrived there, back where she'd started . . .

Because how can the story be a story now, with that sentence – 'She broke from him and ran away . . .'? If she doesn't have them hold each other, this thing happened to both of them, come upon them with great force and now they can't stop it . . . That he would lean down towards her and she reaches up to him and she kisses him. He kisses her. If she doesn't make this moment of them together the start of something dramatic, a confrontation, an embrace, the idea of something momentous beginning, adulterous and powerful and dangerous, and only writes instead about what actually happened that morning, all the details of it that she's put in – then the title is wrong, isn't it? 'Infidelity'?

The story was always to be a real story, a proper story, always that had been her plan. There was to be a woman meeting a man, a stranger, on the first day of her marriage, as had happened – and okay, so perhaps he thought she was someone he already knew . . . That's all fine, that can all stay in. But then, from that, there was something else, an episode that she would imagine that would make the whole thing into fiction, fiction, all made up. So she might start with her morning, from all those years ago, when she went out alone and with barely any clothes on, dressed only to go swimming in the river, to go into that beautiful river, the 'devastating' river, was how she described it . . . So she would start with that. And then . . . And then . . . She would write something different, create an event, an affair, no, not an affair, more of an encounter that took place between a man and a woman one summer's morning, something intense and physical and yes, it would be emotional, too . . . How a new bride was unfaithful on the first day of her marriage. How she could be unfaithful, how she had somehow prepared herself to be: 'Because the next thing she knew, her eyes were open and there was light coming in through the slit between the curtains, through the partly opened window she could hear birdsong, and she was up and dressed, but no shoes on, no underwear.' Remember? So the story might go on from there, but not to this – this other version. How call this 'Infidelity', this thing she's written down here? How infidelity for her theme and content, the very idea behind her story, when nothing, nothing happened at all?

Only that nothing in her life had ever matched it. Not later, when she would hold her firstborn in her arms, or her second and third and fourth, not when she turned, over and over as she would turn, to her husband, in love and desire and comfort . . . Nothing would ever happen to her again that would take such strength, every second of strength in her, in her will, not to yield, and to be able to so break, and run. Nothing else had come close. In all her adult years of planning and striving and thinking, in her long lifetime of being with herself, knowing herself, watching over herself, being so careful with herself, never had this woman, this Helen, had anything come upon her with the same sense of utter shock, of complete and startling unknowingness that yet held for her no fear but was only something she wanted. As though everything else was secondhand, everything in some way planned or imagined or prepared for, her marriage, her children, her life, everything created, like a story, to be thought through and interrogated and organised in advance, and intuited or imagined or already foreseen – only this, a few seconds with a stranger, his fingers encircling her wrist like a bracelet . . . That . . . detail . . .

'It was as though you were waiting for me,' she said.

It came from somewhere else.

So write all that in, Helen, she thinks. Write it in if you can, but how could she? He did nothing, nothing happened between them at all, and yet, in that fragment of time together, every act had been committed, one upon the other. Every want. Desire. Every base and lovely thing. His name had been . . . What was his name? Did he even introduce himself – as he'd stood there before her for those long seconds holding her wrist in his fingers, had he even told her his name? She had barely been able to hear a thing through the surge of her blood.

Helen knows by now she'll have to go back through the story and check some things. Certain words, sentences . . . She has to keep them safe. Write over them, somehow. Write around them – that part about the river, the way she was barely dressed . . . She'll have to be careful how people will read what she's written so far, or how they'll interpret it; she's not sure she can turn large parts of what she's remembered into a story after all. Even if she does make a huge fiction out of it, a big affair and adulterous in intention and effect with the people in it all turned into characters with made up names and faces and lives . . . It's one thing to use the idea of a secret, as a theme, and to have a story, the title of the story, come out of that idea, but it would be wrong to make what happened to her – what really happened, even if it was a long time ago – into a piece of writing for someone else to be curious about, to want to read. It would be wrong, for herself, for her children, her marriage, it would be deeply, deeply wrong.

'Don't go,' he'd called after her as she broke from him and started to run. But she hadn't looked back. He'd waited for her, no doubt, but she did everything in her power not to do that, stop, turn, go back for him.

And so should she submit 'Infidelity' after all, as her contribution to the writing class? Though her professor has told her to take something that happened and 'from these details will come your fiction'. So: The light. The house she stayed in. The flowers in the garden. Though I can see all of this for her, for Helen – and I can put all these details in – I can also see now that writing in this way is not perhaps what Helen wants to do.

'Don't go,' he'd said, but she'd started to run from him by then, she'd started to run.

'Come back!' he shouted after her, but she ran faster and faster and realised as she was running that she was crying, she was sobbing, great wrenching sounds coming out of her like the cries of animals, her whole body racked

with weeping as she ran and she ran, back to that little
cottage she was renting with her husband for their honeymoon, for the first two weeks of their life together. She
ran past the cottage and kept running along the riverbank
and further along the river until it came to the sea and
then she ran along the beach as the waves came in and
she kept running until she could run no more and then
she stopped, finally she stopped, and waited, the crying
stopped, and she turned and slowly, walking now, she
retraced her way back, to the gate of the same little house
where she was staying.

Infidelity.

Over the years, Helen has always thought, she would
tell someone about that morning. About her first day of
married life, the early hour and what had occurred. She's
always thought that one day she might even use it, somehow, write it down as something crafted, that she would
add to it, she means, to make what happened to her into
a fictional account, a long short story about a moment
in the life of a married woman, a newly married woman
– maybe as part of a creative writing class that, with her
youngest about to start secondary school, she has finally
found the time for, where the teacher has told her: 'Detail,
Helen. It's all we have.'

But now that the detail is around her, how could she
ever turn what happened into a story like that? A story
like so many other stories, about love affairs and lies and

sex? How be something that sits apart from her in that way, a particular morning when nothing happened and yet everything had? Louisa may have told her, 'That's how stories are made, Helen. Write every detail down and you'll see. How nothing . . . Becomes everything.' Still, how could Helen ever write that 'everything'? When her husband would read it? Her daughters? Her son? How write that, half an hour later, when she left the beach and returned to the place where she and Richard were staying, there was no sign of the rage of emotions that had passed through her body and mind that morning. That she could go back to the house, through the front gate, walk across the grass again and now the dew had dried upon the lawn. The birds were no longer singing. It was hot and still.

She tries: 'There was the little house,' she writes, 'just as she had left it', but stops. She sits for a few moments, over her pages of sentences and paragraphs, before she scoops them all up and puts them in the bin.

Of course she can't write this story. She was never going to be able to write it.

Instead she opened the door and stepped inside, out of the golden morning and into the darkness. Then, quietly, quietly she went down the shadowed hall to her husband who'd never woken and was still sleeping.

*

Acknowledgements

Stories in this collection have appeared in the following magazines:

'A Story She Might Tell Herself' in *The Kenyon Review*; 'Elegy' in *The Warwick Review*; 'Glenhead' in *Gutter*; 'The Father' in *Granta*; 'Dirtybed' in *The Manchester Review*; 'The Wolf on the Road' in *Five Dials*; 'Tangi' in *The Warwick Review*; 'Dick' in *Open City*.

Also by Kirsty Gunn

ff

The Big Music

As *The Big Music* begins, John Sutherland, an elderly composer, struggles across the vast landscape of the Highlands with ideas for a tune swirling in his head and a baby in his arms. He has taken his newborn granddaughter without permission from her crib – but why? Alarmed by his actions, the Sutherlands gather at their family home, and John's story starts to unfold, intertwined with the history of the house and the great hidden loves it contained, the secrets of families and the music surrounding and defining it all.

'A moving story of fathers, children and a culture in peril.' *Independent* Books of the Year

'A novel of extraordinary unity of purpose . . . Fierce and strange, bleak and beautiful, it is a work that exists entirely, and triumphantly, on its own terms.' *Literary Review*

'It is so rare to read anything so riveting . . . it captivates and illuminates.' *Scotland on Sunday*

ff

The Boy and the Sea

At the start of a summer's day, Ward is waiting on the beach. His friend, Alex, wants him to come to a party at Alison's where there'll be girls and drinks and the possibilities of fun. But Ward is shy and self-conscious and struggling to move from under the weight of his powerful father. He'd rather wait on the beach for the surf to come up. As the sun moves towards its highest point and the girls' laughter carries along the wind towards Ward, the tide changes and Ward is faced with a dramatic event that will change his life forever.

This beautiful and intense coming-of-age story captures perfectly the discomforts and challenges of being fifteen years old with the world stretching out in front of you. Gunn slowly unfolds a tale of danger and sexuality, of mothers and sons and the fathers who rule them, and of the sea.

'It's the drowsy and beguiling poetry of the writing that really matters. Kirsty Gunn's wonderful characterisation of the sea, which suddenly and dramatically turns into a "blue glass mountain" of rising surf, is reason enough to read this book.' *Observer*

ff

Featherstone

Featherstone: an attractive, small rural town serving outlying estates; bank, post office, school . . .

At first glance, Kirsty Gunn's small country town is like any other – a closely connected community bound by habit and familiarity. Yet as we're invited to spend the weekend in Featherstone we come to realise there's something about the place that unsettles us, something intense and intimate that goes deep into the lives of the people who live here and bare their hearts.

'The title of Kirsty Gunn's beautiful new novel is a key – the marvellous weighting of words, how each word falls and floats on the page . . . a richly layered and rewarding novel.' *Scotland on Sunday*